CW00494855

Livingstone's Funeral

LANDEG WHITE

Cinnamon Press
Independent Innovative International

Published by Cinnamon Press
Meirion House, Glan yr afon, Tanygrisiau, Blaenau Ffestiniog, Gwynedd, LL41 3SU
www.cinnamonpress.com

 ISBN 978-1-905614-86-8
British Library Cataloguing in Publication Data. A CIP record for this book can be obtained from the British Library

Designed and typeset in Garamond by Cinnamon Press
Cover design by Mike Fortune-Wood from original artwork 'African Woman with Child statue' by 'Susan Pettitt'; agency: dreamstime.com. Printed and bound in Great Britain by MPG Books Group, Bodmin & King's Lynn.

Cinnamon Press is represented in the UK by Inpress Ltd www.inpressbooks.co.uk and in Wales by the Welsh Books Council www.cllc.org.uk.

The publisher acknowledges the financial support of the Welsh Books Council.

Livingstone’s Funeral

Her genes

encompass history and continents

in a luminous web in which are charmed

men with whom I have nothing in common

beyond our drinking together at weddings.

Where the Angolans are Playing Football

Prologue

The man's heart wasn't in that final homecoming.

For one thing, the route was wrong. Not the long haul he knew backwards round the Cape of Good Hope and up the West Coast, but north to the new canal at Suez which his brain had applauded but which he'd never clapped eyes on. If this seems perverse, I truly believe he was far more a creature of sentiment than of vision.

Then the P&O steamer *Malwa*, which picked up the coffin from the Calcutta at Aden, ran into bad weather soon after Gibraltar and was more than two days overdue when she was at last sighted off Hurst Castle. So instead of landing the reluctant corpse at Netley and sailing on to London, the Malwa had to dock at Southampton to coal.

The plan had been for the cortege to proceed slowly from Netley to Southampton station, with ample opportunity for ceremonials and public grief. But from Southampton docks to the railhead is a miserable two hundred yards.

Moffat, his father-in-law, was there, Oswell, his surviving son, Stanley who made a fortune from finding him when he wasn't lost, Arthur Laing, the merchant who brought the coffin from Zanzibar to Suez and came home a good deal faster, Webb, the hunter and his host at Newstead Abbey, Grant the explorer, Horace Waller the missionary with Jacob Wainwright, the ex-slave now doubly liberated, in tow, together with assorted dignitaries from the Church Missionary Society, the Royal Geographical Society, the Diplomatic Service and the P&O company—all swathed in acres of black cloth and waltzing politely for precedence.

That was the official reception committee, augmented by delegates from a dozen others. But Southampton had bigwigs of its own—his worship the mayor, the town sheriff, the senior and junior bailiffs, aldermen, councillors, the borough magistrates, pier and harbour commissioners, the sitting member—by the time all these personages had been nudged into place on the steaming wet cobbles in front of the hearse, with fellows of the RGS, guardians of the incorporation, clergy and ministers of the town, representatives of the medical profession, committees of the library and philosophical societies and of the Hartley institution, the Southampton school board, consuls of the different nations not to mention family and friends all lined up behind it—well, there was just enough space for everyone present to take two steps forward and there you were at platform one with the engine huffing to steam off to London.

I remark his heart wasn't in it. But the devil was to know just exactly who was in that in that coffin under the Union Jack under the wreath of camellias and immortelles. Or rather, that triple coffin, for this was an affair of Chinese boxes with a zinc-lined coffin of Zanzibar wood painted black by the priests, and inside that a coffin made by the Vulture's carpenter, and inside that the baobab-bark parcel tied together by Susi and Chuma as camouflage, and inside that what precisely?

This was no small matter, I can tell you. What if all the fuss was over some poor Jack Tar or the bones of an Arab slaver? All they had was a box inside two other boxes dispatched from the heart of Africa. What joke was the dark continent playing on them? In the end, it all turned on the word of some poor black fellows whom few in that packed procession would have trusted anywhere near their family silver.

Next morning *The Times* informed us. Stripped of some bright cotton cloth and all medical jargon, it was a four-foot parcel of dry bones. The heart, lungs, intestines and most of the flesh had been removed, and the legs cut from the trunk for easier packaging. The bones were of the requisite number and the skull, at twenty-three and seven-eighths, was the requisite hat size. But the features were unrecognisable and, if this was their man, he had grown his hair and whiskers since he left London. Identification was by an ununited fracture of the left humerus which they all knew had once been chewed by a lion. That six medical men might be mistaken, intoned the Thunderer, was 'beyond human credibility'.

Such vanity over a bag of bones. It seemed little enough to go on. And little enough, in God's name, for Africa to send back after a lifetime's wanderings. But the doctors were probably right. I'd trust Susi and Chuma, and the country was in the mood for a funeral.

I didn't attend the Abbey. I never much liked the man with his all-too-slippery tongue and his Presbyterian self-regard. He nearly ruined Tom Baines's career, and others, with his denial of common justice, and Bishop Mackenzie's death left a nasty smell. You couldn't trust him with authority over Europeans, so why over Africans? Even the slavery business had its distaff side. He hated the trade, no doubt. I don't deny him his passion. 'Open sore of the world' indeed. No man has put it better. Yet he demanded as much, and more, of his own men as any Arab I ever encountered.

That journey to the coast with his body, a thousand miles with a dangerous cargo through countries at war. There's been much talk about 'devotion' with Jacob Wainwright playing the part to perfection. Wainwright's just a clerk in the making. But Susi and Chuma are no fools. They know the man's heart will be forever in Africa, his flesh bonded to the dust he loved, his lungs breathing that quivering air in the black pools of shadow under the acacia trees. If that's what you believe, and they do, and rightly, what's the point of lugging a bundle of bones to Zanzibar? Unless, that is, you're afraid of being called to account.

So the funeral wasn't for me. I read of it just a day or two after the bag of bones piece with all the contradictions banging in my head. For days, the whole English press, the press of the whole civilised world was full of his name. Afterwards, I was sorry to have skipped it for it came to me the occasion wasn't really about the man at all. As I confess I should have foreseen.

It was one of those imperial funerals, those affairs of state that began with the Duke of Wellington's send-off and have been getting grander ever since, whenever a suitable corpse can be found. I blame the widow of Windsor. She's been on the throne so long there's hardly an Englishman under fifty can remember the coronation, and we seem to need these jamborees when, as *The Times* puts it, 'all ranks of the highest and lowest in the land' are brought together for a junket. We have to make do with funerals, being as it were coronations in reverse, reminding the widow yet again of Albert, till the day comes when her own gun carriage is draped in black and King Teddy will have the party of his life.

I must admit it was all very well done, given that the corpse had reached Southampton only three days before. Of course, there'd been advance intelligence from Suez, but they must have been biting their nails when the *Malwa* was storm-bound. Twelve mourning coaches followed the hearse down St James, along Pall Mall past Charing Cross and up Parliament Street, with the widow queen's carriage and forty others in tow. And then the pageant began.

Think of it, the Abbey in full pomp and circumstance, packed from the nave to the giddy clerestory, the sun shining through the choir and lantern windows while the organ pealed and the great bell of St Margaret's tolled—and what had it all to do with the miserable hut he died in after years of wandering in circles?

Think of those pall-bearers chosen, said the Thunderer, as representatives of the three stages of their hero's life. Steele and Oswell for the barren years at Kolobeng where he failed as a missionary and filched all the credit for Oswell's discovery of Lake Ngami. Behind them, Kirk and Waller for all the waste and false promises of the Zambesi fiasco and the cruel deaths through lies and neglect at Magomero and Linyanti. Then, bringing up the rear, Stanley and Wainwright for the futile years wading the muddy springs of a river he denied to his death was the Congo. Was it for this the bitterest enemies in society and politics and religion and science and philanthropy and morals, aye, and diplomacy too (even the Portuguese consul-general was present, grinding his teeth into a forced smile) were all brought together by the need to be seen to be present?

Above all, think of the Abbey choir with picked voices from the Chapels Royal singing Croft and Purcell, and Handel's sublime setting 'His body is buried in peace yet his name liveth for evermore' and those dry bones without heart or brain re-boxed (yet again) in a coffin of English oak.

What was the trick of it? I puzzled as I read those frowsty, overblown columns, wondering if it was envy or middle age or simple patriotism drew from me the angry sarcasm that was my truest emotion.

The truth is Susi and Chuma had done their work too well. They saw their master was pursued by the world, even as far as that hell-hole Ujiji. They saw what happened to Musa and the rascals who deserted him, and they knew their own tale would never be believed without the evidence. So they buried him properly in their own reverential way, and they brought the transportable bits to Zanzibar, to be re-assembled into whatever their masters chose.

What's your deepest desire—the thing you'd climb Everests or paddle Pacifics or labour the seven years of Jacob's bride task for? Is it wealth, power, knowledge, philanthropy, your private paradise? Susi and Chuma brought us these, with the chance to dream their own worlds in the weird continent they walked out of.

All the gold of King Solomon's mines was there, in that Garden of Eden untainted by satanic mills. All human savagery was there, to be tamed by reckless, high-spirited bravery or life-long sacrifice. There Everyman could plant the first footprint, fire the first gun, write his own name in capitals across river, lake and mountain. Everyman could be uncrowned king of the lost tribe, lavish with his favours and worshipped without restraint.

Was it a new science you wanted? The tree of Man traced to its deepest root? Or was your ambition to confirm the holy record in Ararat and Ophir and Meroe? A chance to rebuild the world over again, God-fearing and Bible-punching, in prayer and without liquor? Was it myth and legend inspired you, after a diet of Dickens and George Eliot? Or just freedom from yourselves, freedom to be different from all you have and are, plundering the darkness within you and without, remembering the dark breasts of the velvet-skinned women in the last village you passed?

Susi and Chuma brought all this, freedom to scrawl what's within us across that blank continent the shape of the human heart. Freedom to be born in a cotton-mill, and be buried in the Abbey. And they showed all we'll ever amount to is a bag of dry bones.

Afterwards, for this was the real beginning, afterwards they all poured in—explorers, missionaries, prospectors, big-game hunters, soldiers, map-makers, railway surveyors, traders in rubber, ivory, groundnuts, sesame, beeswax, hippo teeth, indigo, hemp, palm oil, rhino horn, vanilla, crocodile skins, copra, and mangrove bark and labour; diggers of gold, diamonds, silver, emerald, tiger stones, iron, copper and platinum; planters of opium, sugar, sisal, coconuts, tea, tobacco, pyrethrum, palm oil, coffee and citrus; Baptists, Dominicans, Methodists, Franciscans, high church, low church, Benedictines, Presbyterians, Trappists, Congregationalists, Seventh Day Adventists, Plymouth Brethren, Jehovah's Witnesses and Mary's Oblates; botanists, taxidermists, phrenologists, evolutionists, journalists, anthropologists and folklorists; colonial governors, commissioners, residents and collectors; judges and policemen.

A few, like Mary Kingsley, went to Africa in search of a death.

Major Geoffrey Clunies-Roland (retired)
The King's Shropshire Light Infantry

Rainmaker

'The world is not as it is. Angels trumpet from its four corners.'

The Reverend Albert Toyne had written this in his leather bound diary, his sister's gift, the evening he first glimpsed Zanzibar after the voyage from Cape Town in the cramped frigate. His spidery copperplate lay before him, a little smudged on the damp page, under the date October 2, 1880, and he tried to remember what inspired them. Had it been his first glimpse from the harbour of the tower of Christ Church Cathedral newly built on the old slave market? That would look good in print, read out at a Mission meeting. But Toyne tried hard to be an honest man and, in fact, all he could remember were the flat green swamplands of the coast with its great brown rivers. Then after dark, when the land breeze stopped, the night air warm as a cloth, smelling of salt and urine.

He had written nothing since. He couldn't write on the march, needing a proper desk or at least a table like the one Smart had knocked together for him in his brand new house. But now at Migodo, two hundred miles inland and ignoring the passage of nine weeks, he continued writing clearly and urgently.

'It disturbs me that they came again today. There were more of them than before, all the chiefs and headmen of the district. One fellow wore brass rings and bangles with his long hair done in greasy plaits. Chuma says he is from the lakeshore. He never once looked me in the face and kept humming an odd little tune and pretending to be preoccupied. I don't trust that man. Chuma says they have been waiting until the house was finished. Until the boys had done the thatching, he says, they knew there was no point in asking.

'But I've seen them often. Themba and Kuwali have been here nearly every day.'

'They come to see the house, bwana father. These illiterate people never see any square house. They come to watch it fall down.'

Chuma spat derisively. I hate it when he behaves as though he has learned nothing from his years with us. It is true their huts are round and uncomfortable. Their village sprawls like an accident and they know nothing of straight lines.

'It's a month since they first came to ask. It was November.'

'Yes, bwana. But next day we did fix the corner posts, isn't it? Then we build the frame and the women plaster the walls and the boys finishing the thatch. So they asking again.'

That is what disturbs me. I can see their logic. There's no sense in asking a man to make rain when he's building his house. Even in Christ's parable of the house built on sand, the rains came only after it was finished. But where's the logic in asking me to make rain? I pray God we are building on the rock. I refused to talk with the chiefs. When I do talk with them I want to be taking the initiative. Chuma says they will be here again tomorrow and the next day and the next until they have persuaded me. We shall see about that.

The rains must be here soon. Every afternoon it gets hotter and hotter and black clouds pile up from the coast. I imagine them tracking us, following the route of our caravan inland and stopping overhead. But then nothing happens. We wait, looking upwards. After dusk, through my neat square window and open square doorway I can see the electric storm. Every few seconds it lights up the heavens, a dazzling shock blue while great forks of lightning spread like the branches of a winter oak. The mountain between here and the lake looms incredibly black, with a fringe of stunted trees like hairs bristling on a sleeping monster. Even at midnight, the heat is stifling and my skin runs with perspiration.

Little do the chiefs know how much I too am longing for the rains. If I knew the trick of bidding them, I would gladly chant my spells. God willing, the day will come when I can bear witness against their superstitions.

Our tiny party has been settled here for almost six weeks. We are a priest (*mea culpa!*), a catechist (Chuma), a cook (Banda) and a jack-of-all-trades called Smart who was born and bred in Glasgow and whose conversation I can scarcely understand. I keep wanting to call him Jock though his baptised name is Thomas. I have to admit his Swahili advances much faster than mine does. He seems to hear the language while I must write the words in my vocabulary book before I can fix them in my head. He and Chuma have great jabbering sessions while I still have to talk to my catechist in English. Jock is employed to teach the natives carpentry, tanning, brick making, printing and whatever else he has picked up in his varied life. He claims he once worked in a pharmacy in Trinidad and we have put him in charge of our medicine chest.

Our caravan was a small one, twenty-nine porters and a gun bearer, all recruited by Chuma in Zanzibar from his long experience (he was with Thompson, you know, as well as with Captain Phipson-Wybrants when he died.) But you would have laughed to see our bundles. We had a dozen boxes (mainly tinned food and glass beads), bolts of white and indigo calico, three carpet bags (you remember my sky blue one with the claret stain), our medicine chest (which Jock Smart never once took his eyes off), two sacks jangling with pots and pans (which though they were the lightest were unpopular because they were hard to balance on woolly heads), two battered suitcases Chuma bought years ago in India and has carried everywhere since (including England; please excuse all these parentheses) and last, but certainly not least, my precious cork bed, the greatest of luxuries and weighing a mere seven pounds *avoirdupois*.

You wouldn't think we looked in any way intimidating but it is a fact we met not a soul for a whole week. That there were people around I was sure of. Occasionally, we caught half a glimpse of a dark figure scuttling into the tall grass or peering from behind the boulders of the hilltops. But their gardens were deserted and whenever we came to a village it was empty behind its wooden palisades.

At last, Banda brought an old man to us. The result of the interview was the purchase of some fowls and vegetables for half a fathom of white calico, a promise on the part of the native that he would tell his neighbours we are good Englishmen and merciful, and an attempt to express to him that we had come to teach the black people about God and Commerce.

I was not entirely satisfied that the message had been understood. Jock muttered audibly about 'good Englishmen' and I must say I see his point. We are a motley company. But Chuma, who is perfectly happy to be 'English', looked very pleased. Immediately, he took one of the guns and ran off into the long grass. Within fifteen minutes, he had shot a large antelope. The result was a long night of drumming and feasting and, I fear, some drinking by our porters of a thick native concoction which appeared in baskets from nowhere, followed by a whole day's halt while everyone recovered their senses. From then onwards, we had no difficulty. I need to remember always that God is our help and that we attempt nothing in our own name.

We reached Migodo in just twenty-four days with not a single package or bundle missing. We even have one extra, by the bye, a box of distress rockets from the Albatross which somehow got mixed up with our own. I pray God they don't think we missionaries are thieves. It was mainly Chuma's doing. He managed it well, kindly in the Livingstone fashion, not like Henry Morton Stanley with his whips and scorpions.

But you don't need me to tell you about Chuma. I confess it is not easy supervising a legend. No one, not even Susi and Amoda, has been with the mission longer. He was adopted as a child by our Pioneer Martyr and his faithful service to our great example Livingstone has become a legend. His claims are great. But he is a black man notwithstanding. Were he an old man like Banda, my position would be much easier. But he is still frivolous at thirty-two and even his wife's death doesn't seem to have depressed his spirits. He calls me 'bwana father' or sometimes just 'bwana' with the smile of a man who has served many bwanas. 'I am in books' he told me once during our journey here. I should have rebuked him at once but I was frankly dumbfounded and by the time I had collected my thoughts he was laughing again as if it were all a great joke.

I doubt the wisdom of making him catechist. He is not exactly cheeky or disloyal but he is disturbingly high-spirited. He knows too well how dependent I am upon him in a wild country where I speak very little of the language. He was always at his best under Susi's firm leadership—as during the sad caravan to Zanzibar with great Livingstone's mortal remains. He talks much of England and Newstead Abbey and Mr Waller.

As for Banda, he is an utter mystery. He is an old man for this part of the world where few people live beyond two score years. He calls Chuma 'master'. That is his only

English word and if he speaks Swahili it is very different from the language I have been studying. His meals, too, are in some strange dialect my stomach has not yet learned to comprehend. But my humour is unworthy. Banda, too, is a child of God and his eagerness to please in all things is touching.

You must not take these characterisations too seriously. I am far from home in a strange and savage place with three such dependants as I never before encountered.

Chuma drew for the chiefs a squiggling line in the dirt.

'Madzi,' he said. 'The stream,' he added for Smart's benefit.

'I ken that much, mon,' Smart muttered.

Chuma drew the path from the stream uphill to the village. Then hastily, with deft twirls of his stick, he sketched in a dozen or so houses along the curve of the hillside.

'Mudzi,' he announced. 'The village'.

The chiefs looked at each other suspiciously. There were twenty-two of them, assembled from the highlands and the lakeshore. They had expected to be speaking with Father Toyne but the white man was taking his siesta. Kuwali made to speak but Chuma silenced him with a wave of his left hand while he continued drawing houses. Then carefully, at the head of the village, he outlined a small rectangle and gave it a gabled roof.

'Nyumba Bwana Toyni. Father Toyne's house'

There was a sigh of comprehension followed by an outburst of relieved laughter. Chombe, the old man from the village across the valley, came to stand beside Chuma, stroking his beard as he studied the picture from that angle.

'Nyumba Bwana Toyni,' he confirmed, nodding his head vigorously and there was more laughter.

Only Kathupa with his long hair and bangles refused to join in. He had walked a long way to this meeting. His village was thirty miles from Migodo, on the shore of the inland lake. It was not on any of the normal trade routes to the coast but it was important because of its two lagoons. The first, all-but cut off from the lake by a sandbar, was famous for its fish, a type of carp called chambo. The second, fed by a stream from the mountain, was completely cut off except during the rainy season. Its waters were saline and soil of its banks, barren except for a few stunted mangrove trees, were rich in salt.

Despite these resources, which made him an important chief, Kathupa was afraid of drought. He was a child when the white man they called Doroti passed through his village. Some people called him Listonia and others Narki, but Dotori was the name he remembered. It must have been Dotori because Chuma had been with him. It was his uncle Mutumbe who ruled then. He and his hunters had just killed a hippopotamus outside the fish lagoon when the white man's safari arrived. Kathupa could remember his uncle being lectured about the slave trade, and how to grow cotton, and how angry he had been. Dotori wanted to cross the lake but none of the traders would help him with their dhows because of the things he said about them in England. That was how dangerous he was. In the end, Dotori had to walk to Maponda's and cross the river at the end of the lake by canoe.

You couldn't avoid the slavers. They had guns and many men. But you could keep out of their way and avoid offending them by giving them two or three people a year—the thieves, the adulterers, the witches. Most of all, you could avoid offending the ancestors as those other white men had done by fighting to take over the country and then not offering prayers or pouring libations of millet beer. The last time missionaries came there was a drought worst than the droughts of legend, the drought they called magumanya when people died in their heaps and he, Kathupa, had buried two wives.

In his heart of hearts, Kathupa was far from sure the white men had caused the drought. It was true they had failed to take the proper precautions, but the ancestors were not stupid and they knew these strangers were ignorant of their ways. But since the slave trade had come, when Mutumbe was a boy, there had been so much fighting and so much movement of peoples. No one knew whose ancestors were the most important these days, and perhaps even the ancestors were fighting among themselves.

In the old days, no one died just because the rains had failed. There was always food somewhere, roots and grasses and tubers in the bush which the old women knew how to prepare. But droughts changed the balance of power, and it took wisdom to manage those changes. That was why the last drought had turned to magumanya, because the white men had used their guns unwisely. They had joined in the wars and started raiding for themselves.

From what he had seen of Bwana Toyni, he had no confidence things would be better this time.

Kathupa gave Chuma's diagram the briefest of glances before turning away and feeling in his long robes for his pipe and a length of coiled tobacco. With studied nonchalance he bit off a knuckle's length and shredded it into the bowl, calling to a little boy squatting at the edge of the meeting to bring him a stick from the fire.

Chuma waited patiently. He had caught their attention, making the occasion his own, and he knew that the meeting's expectancy would soon bring Kathupa into line. He added tiny details to his drawing such as the three granaries within Chief Themba's compound and the bwalo or meeting place where they were all sitting under a giant fig tree, until he could see that Kathupa was puffing furiously.

Then he called out, 'Banda!'

'Master!'

The old man hobbled forward, bowing and holding his fingertips together in a gesture of obeisance.

'Chisesu,' ordered Chuma.

Banda looked bewildered but, when the order was repeated, began talking very quickly in a falsetto whisper to the little boy who had taken the burning stick to Kathupa. The child ran off on spindly legs, returning with a stick broom which he handed to Banda, who carried it forward and gave it to Chuma. Then the old man retreated behind the fig tree, walking backwards and again touching his fingertips.

Chuma looked at the broom and looked at his drawing in the dirt. Imperiously, with half a dozen measured strokes, he swept Migodo away leaving only the stream and Toyne's house. Then carefully, with a short stick, working from the plans Toyne had shown him but which in truth he knew by heart from his childhood, he drew a church with a square tower at the head of the village just beyond Toyne's house. Next he drew a schoolhouse divided into four classrooms to the right of the space in front of the church and, across the way, two dormitories for the boys and the girls. He added houses, slightly smaller than Toyne's, for the school master and school mistress, a meeting house immediately opposite Toyne's rectory, and finally a line of square houses with neat gardens along each side of an avenue curving between the face of the hillside and the stream.

It took him some time, partly because the chiefs were crowding around him blocking his light so that he had shoo them away impatiently, but partly too because it was a labour of love.

Chuma was a child when the first bishop rescued him from the slavers. He had no means of knowing how old he had been since he no longer had a family and he could remember very little before that time. Sometimes he thought his memories were only what the missionaries had told him but sometimes they felt real. He was sure he remembered the slave gang, marching for week after week with his wrists tied and his neck in the goree, the forked stick, so that when you tripped or stumbled through tiredness you nearly choked. Mr Waller had cut him free and they had made a fire with the sticks and cooked massa. He was almost sure he remembered this, but he had seen to many different pictures of it, some in colour and some in black and white, some with his face and some of them unrecognisable, that he couldn't any longer be certain.

What he did remember was the next two years, serving the white men with Wekotani and Chinsoro. Chinsoro was dead now. He was shot for no reason by that angry man Mr Faulkner, with the red face. Mr Waller would be very angry when he heard and perhaps he would make a case of it. But Wekotani had turned his back on the white men and gone home to his village. He told Dotori Livingstone, 'No bwana, I am staying here,' when they were crossing the end of the big lake. He say, 'These are my people.' You could see the Dotori was very angry but there was nothing he could say because he was against slaves. Wekotani was not his slave, not his slave, but he was stupid, very stupid ungrateful boy, but Wekotani say, 'These are my people.'

So he stay there at the lakeshore close by Mponda's. Chuma sighed loudly, wishing he could see his friend again. If you don't have relatives you are a slave. Chuma knew this was true and he had made the white men his family. There was a woman once who says she is my mother's sister, same father different mother, and I want to give her some beads but Dotori Livingstone say, 'No, Chuma. How you can be so stupid to let these wicked people steal from you?' So Dotori say 'No, Chuma,' and I make the bwana my family.

It wasn't a safe life because the bishop and Mr Waller were so much fighting with Kalinga and Mlumbe and the others, and it wasn't comfortable because everything was so strange. He wore a grey shirt and khaki shorts and he had to put the knife and fork in the right places and the napkin on the right side with the glass.

As he sketched the mission settlement in the dust with the chiefs studying every detail, he felt his eyes stinging. What he was drawing was the only happy time. After that he had to go to India, to Dotori Wilson who made him a Christian and called him James. James Chuma, born at Kusogwe, son of Chimilengo, fisherman, and Chinjeriapi, housewife. That was what was written on his baptismal certificate. Long afterwards at Newstead, Mr Waller told him what a housewife was. He wished he could remember his father, the fisherman and his mother, the housewife. To have no relatives makes you weep.

Then Dotori Wilson gave him back to Dotori Livingstone and for six years he just walking with the Dotori. The white men could be so stupid, walking, walking, walking, and for what? The Dotori gave him a wife, Ntaoeka, when they were in Manyema. But with a wife you want to stop walking. You want to build a house and start planting and have children. But no, Chuma and Ntaoeka start walking and walking again. And then Dotori Livingstone dies and we make proper funeral and it all finish. But no, Susi says, 'We must walk to Dotori's people.' So we carry the box with Ntaoeka walking and it all finish up in England in Newstead Abbey with Mr Waller and the big book.

So this time Chuma, James Chuma, son of Chimilengo, fisherman and Chinjeriapi, housewife, decide to earn money, big money. He decide to become a big man like Bombay with many servants, or like Ali Kiongwe. Chuma sniggered despite himself, because he remembered that Kiongwe's name meant 'stupid jackass', so everyone, when he become a rich man, have to call him Shaongwe instead which is more polite, but Kiongwe was his real name and it mean 'jackass'. So Chuma worked with Bwana Thompson and that was walking, walking once more but good good money with Chuma head man in the caravan. And then come disaster. He take service as caravan leader with Kapitini Phelps who want to fight with the Portuguese on the Sabi River. But the Portuguese make big witchcraft to keep their land. So the Kapitini die of fever and then Ntaoeka die as well and Chuma, James Chuma, understand his situation.

Only the mission was his family. He could not break free and be a man himself on his own.

The last detail of his picture in the dust was a house for himself. He drew another rectangle, sub-divided into three rooms, and with a gabled roof. Then he added other features—a dovecot on a pole, a hen house, a kitchen where Banda would work with a round hut for his quarters, and a vegetable plot, not for his main crops (his farm would be in the dambo or marshlands in the valley) but for his special plants: a square of hemp for smoking and a plot of chili peppers to take with his relish.

With a flourish, he signed his name 'James Chuma' at the bottom of the sketch. He had written his name on the village. That was how you did it. There was a mountain called Mr Waller and a whole range of mountains called

Mr Kirk. You saw it and you like it and you write it down in a book. Then you have your place.

He sat back on his haunches, breathing heavily. Then he stood up and prepared to harangue the chiefs about commerce and progress.

But Kathupa was too furious to listen.

'You Kalisti people,' he shouted. 'You tie up the rains!'

He paced across the bwalo as though to strike Chuma, then swirled round suddenly so that his robes brushed Chuma's knees, and pointed to the black clouds overhead with an open palm.

'Last time,' he declared. 'In our fathers' day. You all saw it. There was famine, magumanya, heap upon heap. You remember your children dying. Do I speak truly?'

Themba sighed deeply and the chiefs gave their assent. As Kathupa continued his speech he kept pausing, on a rising cadence, and his audience responded with grunts of 'Eh-eh' and 'Chabwino'.

'That was war,' Chuma interrupted impatiently. 'You people always fighting.'

'It was magumanya,' said Kathupa. I had two wives, Asawilunda and Akaswiri. They both died with their children. Why are you bringing these white people back again? Again, they tie up the rains.'

He grabbed the broomstick and with a single curving stroke drove a cyclone through Chuma's village.

But he had gone too far. The chiefs had come with a petition and they had not yet seen Bwana Toyni. They were not ready for a fight. They were not even hostile to Chuma, who was just a foolish young man, and they had been intrigued by his drawing.

Chuma watched, biting his lip in annoyance as the meeting broke up inconclusively. Then he, too, turned on his heel and left the bwalo without courtesies or farewell.

Smart caught up with him on the stony track back to the house they still shared.

He joked roughly.

'So, you's to have a nice little compound? A house for you. A house for you's new wife. Cook house. Hen house. Granary. Latrine. Vura nice.'

Chuma turned on him where the path curved round the hillside. Smart was astonished by his vehemence.

'I see your country. I see your big country. Big houses, big palaces, big men. I want to walk into my house like a man, not an animal on four legs.'

He stalked ahead through the village. Smart could set from the set of his shoulders he was sulking.

For the first time in nine weeks Toyne felt close to his sister Agnes. When his mother died it was she, at thirteen, who became mother of the six year old orphan. His father, the archdeacon, had been a remote figure in his book-lined study. Then, when his fiancé died of tuberculosis, it was Agnes who came closest to consoling him. She understood his wish to bury himself in Africa, Her gift of a diary was her only claim on him.

'You must keep a journal. Like a real explorer.'

He was developing the habit of writing it up at first light, after cockcrow and prayers but before walking down to the stream to bathe. He had begun his account nine weeks in arrears and he found it less disturbing to maintain the distance of a night's sleep between his experiences and the record. Sometimes he left things out, recording them days later when they had begun to fall into the pattern.

This had begun with the renewal of order when he awoke for the first time in his own house. It was a relief to escape from the hut Themba the headman had given him when they first came to Migodo. It wasn't only the darkness and the fleas, the rats scampering along the rafters, and the smell of former occupants, of stewed beans and wood smoke. There was nowhere to fit a bookshelf. He lived in a narrow circle, unable to get his bearings. For six weeks he had kept his prayer book and Christian Year in a cracked water pot opposite the door. But this wasn't something he had yet told his diary. He had seen enough of the villagers to know that they too kept their household spirits in clay pots.

So it was a joy to wake up in his cork bed alongside a straight wall in a room with a table and chairs, a bedside cabinet for his shaving kit, his sister's photograph, and the clock with the alarm (why in the name of goodness bring that to Migodo with its thousand cockerels?), and a set of shelves rigged up by Smart for his small library: *The Imitation of Christ*, *The Dream of Gerontius*, Bowdler's Shakespeare, Palgrave's *Golden Treasury*, and (a gift from his sister, the pages so far uncut) *Middlemarch*. On the table was current reading, his *Bible* and prayerbook and a dog-eared copy of the two volumes of *The Last Journals of David Livingstone*.

Without conscious planning, their days fell into Toyne's timetable, rising at seven to bathe in the deserted stream, followed by prayers and breakfast at eight-thirty and a morning spent doing what Toyne described as 'settling in'. During these hours there were few people around. The village men were up before dawn, leaving for the fields while the women, splashing their faces with water from the tall pots, stayed only to light fires with pots of beans or pigeon peas before they followed their husbands to work, their babies folded snug on their backs. By the time Toyne and Smart were about the village was deserted, except for the girls left in charge of the cooking pots and the very small children playing. Sometimes the girls would bring fresh water from the streams or take the children off into the tall grass to play at home-making. But by midday, when the missionaries lunched, even the children had gone off with the cooking pots to the family farms and the village was quite empty.

Sometimes, not taking his customary siesta, Toyne wandered round the silent village he had chosen as the centre of the region's redemption. He was a little surprised by his sudden passion for town planning. He had never built anything, and without Smart would have been quite helpless in his constructions. But in this new landscape, he could make nothing of nothing. There were thirty-nine compounds in Migodo (counting was easy when the village was deserted), each one consisting of separate huts for the men and their wives with various out-houses for cooking, storing grain and keeping chickens. But he couldn't work out why Migodo was where it was or why the compounds were distributed as they were.

It was not a stockaded village like the ones they had passed coming up from the coast. It was built on a narrow shelf of land between the valley where most people had their farms and the hill where they took refuge at times of trouble. It was actually this hill which was called Migodo. Toyne had climbed up there on his second day and had found crevices on the granite summit which were packed with human bones. The view from the top had given him no clues. He had expected to see jungle with herds of wild animals, and on the journey from the coast had kept postponing this expectation. Now on arrival he looked out across a sloping yellow-brown plain with scattered upside-down trees and strange conical hills topped with black boulders. It was easier to imagine it had been abandoned by its former inhabitants as being of no further use to them than as a place of present and future hopes. Villages sprouted here and there like clusters of thick grey mushrooms, and turquoise creases marked the courses of perennial streams. On the horizon was the mountain, fringed again with Y-shaped trees, which divided the plain from the lakeshore.

By mid-afternoon, the village began to fill. First, the women came back from the farms to wash and fill their water pots, spreading flour to dry and filling the air with the songs and the thump-thump of their pounding. Then the men ambled back carrying their iron hoes, collecting to smoke in the bwalo while they waited for the evening meal. At dusk, despite the storm clouds, the village was bathed in yellow light. Every compound was marked by cooking fires, the children crowding round their mothers, demanding stories or a lick of the ladle.

At this time, almost daily, Toyne felt wretched in his shyness, unable to communicate and ridiculous in all his plans. He was rescued by Banda with the summons to dinner followed by prayers and Bible study and an hour's wrestling with the language.

Only on Sundays could he seize the initiative. So far he had refused to preach, a measure of his distrust of Chuma who could have interpreted for him. Instead, he sang Matins at nine, intoning the Scriptures and singing the hymns, his voice (which even he felt was unfortunately parsonical) resounding between the deserted huts and making the farmers in the valley feel uneasy. Some of them crept back to watch from a safe distance. Seeing his advantage, Toyne made the service increasingly elaborate, with robes and incense and, most recently, Holy Communion for Chuma, Smart and Banda. For the last two Sundays, Evensong had been a triumph. With the day's work done, Evensong in the bwalo with prayers by Toyne and a Scripture reading by Chuma had become as popular as a village dance, not just for Migodo but for the villages across the stream. Twice now, with up to five-hundred people watching in complete silence, Toyne had felt released from all his doubts and hesitations.

'But still,' he wrote, 'it has not rained. Chuma says the chiefs are becoming angry.'

'It was my last night in the hut before I moved to my house. I awoke just after midnight in a cold sweat, though the heat was as oppressive as ever, and lit my lamp. I saw it straightaway, a snake up on the rafter, its tiny cat's eyes shining, its tongue flickering in a way that made me shudder. I won't deny I was very frightened. I got out of bed slowly and backed along the wall to the door while the snake stared at the yellow flame. Outside, it was pitch black with no a single star, but my shouts brought Banda running. He took one look at the snake and disappeared, but returned at once carrying a twist of some kind of root or herb and blowing hard on a stick from the fire.

'When he held the root to the glowing embers the hut was filled with a strange odour like a mixture of camphor and incense. The snake lifted its head several times. Then it turned and disappeared through the gap under the eaves. Banda left the stick with the substance on the floor and the gentle smell remained as I fell asleep.'

Writing this five days afterwards, he was struck by another memory. Banda had bowed with his hands together and said something like 'Bo noyti, bwana.'

Extinguishing his oil lamp and lying in the darkness, Toyne had wondered. What language was Banda speaking? Could it have been Portuguese?

'This evening,' wrote Toyne long after midnight, breaking his habit, 'it was Chuma's turn to select the Old Testament reading. Unhappily, his choice fell on I Kings 18, verses 17 to 46. You know the passage, about Elijah and the prophets of Baal and the cloud that appeared no bigger than a man's hand. It set off an argument I regretted.

'"Sometimes," I tried to explain to Chuma, "the Bible must be read in a sense that is not literal. This is especially true when reading the Old Testament which came before the fuller revelation in the Gospels. The prophetic books must be read historically. That is because they anticipate the greater truths of the New Testament. They must be read symbolically, as prefiguring the incarnation in Christ Jesus our Lord. And they must be read intelligently, since God has planted reason in our minds. This means disregarding anything that conflicts with the further revelations of science."

'It is not often I hit off phrases that encapsulate exactly what I believe and I must admit I was pleased with my eloquence.

'"So you see, Chuma, although Elijah defeated the prophets of Baal by bringing rain, that was because he lived in superstitious times. In general, symbolic terms, the God of Judah was much greater than the gods of the hilistines. But in practice, such"—I had to search for the right word—"such tournaments between gods have very little to do with religious truth. Scientifically, they are nonsense. God does not control the rains any more than he is to be blamed for earthquakes or thunderbolts."

'Chuma was silent for a few minutes.

'"What is tournament?" he asked.

'"Jousting. A competition. Like a wrestling match."

'Chuma was truly distressed. His forehead was creased both horizontally and vertically and he was wringing his hands in agitation.

'"Books," he said. "In books there is only truth. That is why there is writing. God is word, written down. Chained to paper. Otherwise, you just have words flying. Doing damage, like bad spirits at night. Like witches' spells."

'"All books?" I exclaimed.

'"Writing," said Chuma. "In the beginning was the Word."

'So here I was in the heart of Africa, plunged into the Essays and Reviews controversy. It amuses me that my problem was the opposite of Bishop Colenso's. I was no Evangelical, defending the literal inspiration of the Divine Record against sceptical Zulus who knew the story of Noah's Ark could not possibly have happened as Moses describes it.

'"How did they keep the leopards and zebras apart?" they asked him, and poor Colenso, with his diagrams drawn in the dirt, was lost for a reply.

'No, I was a Tractarian under attack from a fundamentalist.

'I was rescued by Smart.

'"Nay, nay mon," he said. "Nay, Chuma, my friend. Ye canna say all books are true. Have ye no heard of Gulliver's Travels? About the little people and the big people. It's very interesting and funny an a'. But it's nae true."

'Chuma looked blank.

'"You don't believe the Holy Bible?" he asked Smart.

'"Oh, aye, the guid book. That's a different matter," said Smart.

'So I was on my own.

'I do wish it would rain for a day or two and resolve our little problem. Night after night the electric storms continue, sending their antlers of lightning high into the dark sky above the bristling mountain. I perspire perpetually and even to maintain this diary I have to keep a handkerchief under my wrist to prevent soiling the page before I have written on it. I have even felt tempted to offer a prayer or two. How easy it must be to be low Church. Lay everything upon God. But God gave us reason to use to His glory. I could not pray with faith, only credulity, and why should He answer except to mock my little faith?

'But I was curious about one thing. I said to Chuma, "What did your master do?"

'"He follow the Holy Bible in all things. He read it from end to end, end to end, he never stop. He tell talk about Moses and Egypt, and about the Nile and Meroe, and about Philip the Evangelist and the Ethiopian, one black man who run with God to Africa. Ethiopia shall raise her voice to God. And about Jonah and the whale and about King David and the Shulamite woman. When he in bad trouble, bad trouble like Bambare in Manuyema, where he give me my wife Ntoeka, he take the Holy Bible and he take his key, the key of his big chest, and he shut both his eyes and he stick the key to mark one page, and when he open his eyes he reads it to us what it say just there. Blessed are they who hunger and thirst. And he tells us, 'You faithless Africans! That is why we go hungry tonight. That is why we find no massa tonight. Because the Lord bless us.'"

'Before he was a quarter into this speech, I realised he was talking not of the beloved Bishop, our martyr, but of Dr Livingstone.

'"Aye," said Smart. "My ain grandmother did likewise. She would take the house key and the family Bible and mark us a text for the day. I used to wonder she never ripped the fine paper."

'At another moment, such colourful folklore would have charmed me. But this had the air of a small crisis.

'"Are you telling me Dr Livingstone used to pray for rain?"

'Chuma smiled in that superior manner of his, shaking his head.

'"No, bwana father. The Doroti never still in one place. He never build a house. He always walking, walking. Only in Bambare when his feet too sore with ulcers, and then was already raining too much."

'"What about the bwana Bishop?"

'"Bishopi?"

'"Our blessed martyr."

'"Eeeh!"

'Chuma composed himself, ready to tell a story. I recognised the signs. He clasped his fingers and pursed his thick lips as though endowed with the wisdom of the ages.

'"The Bishopi say, Bible is not one book. Bible is many book. They all true but they all true differently."

'This was sound enough. In fact, I thought it was more or less what I had been telling Chuma. However, he continued.

'"One day we talking about Black men. Why God create ugly black men. I tell him, the Bible say is the mark of Cain. Is God's punishment for killing Abel. Abel is one day sitting at his desk like an Englishman, writing a report, when Cain rush in like a madman from his farm, all covered in dirt, and chop him dead with a cutlass. So Cain become the first Black man."

'"When he hear me say this, the Bishopi smile a little to heself and write something in his notebook. Then he smile again and he say, 'Nonsense, Chuma, nonsense. All that happen long long time ago, long before Noah and the Flood, when the human race and all the animals start over again, two by two. The Bible no say anything about White man and Black man in Noah's arc. They just mankind.' So then I understand, Bible is many book, but they all true differently."

'I found this story intensely moving. I imagined the conversation taking place after prayers, around the fireside outside that primitive hut which was his only palace in Africa. Theologically, it was irreproachable, even from the Evangelical viewpoint. But how well the Bishop had understood how to adapt his teaching to the level of his hearers. God give me grace to match his humility.

'"But did the Bishop ever prayer for rain?"

'Chuma looked at me sharply.

'"He dead, sah, before the first rains come."

'I was shocked. I had known his labours in the field had been brutally cut short. But I had forgotten he had died before the first rains.'

Even before the news broke, Smart knew something was wrong. He was up at four-thirty as usual, and walked down to the stream to inspect the dam.

The dam was Toyne's idea.

'Think of it,' he had exclaimed, fired with the enthusiasm of the amateur. 'We could mill flour for the whole mission. Make electricity. Pump water up the hill the whole year round. Have taps and standpipes. No more of this nonsense about making rain.'

This morning, Smart descended the path alone and when he got to the stream he found several of the boulders displaced. The damage was half-hearted and took no more than an hour to put right. It was the absence of interested spectators that worried him.

Back at the village, he found Toyne distraught.

Banda had disappeared overnight. There had been no morning prayers, and there was no breakfast.

Smart went into the blackened hut behind Toyne's manse which served as Banda's kitchen and soon produced a handsome tray of tinned ham lightly fried with eggs and a jug of coffee. But Toyne was inconsolable. Banda had been killed. Banda had been sold into slavery. It was their duty to rescue him.

'No, bwana father,' said Chuma. 'He just go freely. He take all his things.'

All his things? How much, Smart wondered, did Banda own?

'He take his two shirt,' said Chuma. 'He take his knife and his mat.'

'So he's not been kidnapped. Did he take any food?'

Banda was in charge all of their stores.

'Let's talk with Themba,' said Smart. 'He'll know what's afoot.'

Toyne brightened visibly. One of his deepest frustrations was the absence of a secular power to handle questions like this. He longed to be, like St Augustine, the spiritual head of a body politic, with powers which were clearly demarcated. Render unto Caesar Caesar's things and unto God, God's. This morning, it was easier to think of Banda as Caesar's business.

As usual, the village was deserted. Even the children had gone.

'Come on, mon,' said Smart. 'We'll go speak with Themba.'

Something about Chuma's reluctance made Smart suspicious. At least, Toyne was upset. Chuma seemed nonchalant about the cook's disappearance. As he and Chuma set off for Themba's farm, he challenged the catechist directly.

'Look here, mon. Don't play buggers with me. If there's trouble, out wi' it.'

Chuma grunted. He spat carefully to his left, then glanced at Smart and began speaking swiftly in Swahili. Smart could understand only part of it, but he interrupted with questions and the picture slowly became clear. It concerned Kathupa. Kathupa's people had been praying for rain. They had danced chopa, the men stamping in a circle with spears and axes in their hands, even with snakes around their necks, while the women danced in the opposite direction bearing green branches. They prayed to Mutumbe, Kathupa's uncle. They built a house over his grave. Kathupa's sister went into the hut to offer libations of millet beer. Then she came out and walked round it three times. Three times this way and three times that way, scattering water from a pot and praying to Mutumbe, 'Send us rain, send us rain.'

Smart nodded slowly. Chuma reverted to English.

'There come big lightning cock and smash her dead.'

'Holy Christ!' said Smart.

'Big lightening *pu-PA!wawawa!* and she dead there on the ground with her waist beads scattered, and everyone seeing.'

'Ah, Jesus! The poor woman.'

'Ah, Jesu Kalisti.'

'So what did Kathupa do?'

'He promise he go find out who did this bad thing.'

'You were telling this to the Reverend?'

'Yes, I tell the bwana father. First, he no believe me. He say I lying about the rain. Then he believe me, and say yes, that why they kill Banda. Then he no believe me again.'

Aye, thought Smart. So the Reverend's in a panic.

'But Banda ken this?'

'He hear it all last night. Then he tell me. Then he leave.'

Smart had had many jobs in many places but he had never given them much thought. He did them well since competence was important to him. But he had no vision of himself as a maker whose work affected other people. He had thought it would be interesting to come to Africa when the reverend running the Mission to Seamen in Liverpool told him there was a job in Zanzibar. 'A need', the reverend had called it. This had happened when the widow that Smart was interested in had married a strapping Negro from Demerara. So he signed on with the mission for three years. Not broken hearted by any means. Just a change of scenery.

He had no regrets. This was a fine country, warm, agreeable and fertile. He liked the people and especially the women, going about their affairs bare-breasted and businesslike without any concern for staring in mirrors. So far as he could make out, their villages were sensible affairs. In a place where most living was done outside, he could see little wrong with the houses. Or huts, as Toyne and Chuma kept calling them. He had an eye for design and could see that if bamboo, grass and mud were the best materials you'd to hand, the houses were pretty well the right shape. He reckoned most of the time these black fellows knew what they were about.

Which is why his job had begun to worry him. He had expected to be doing all the mission's practical business—building a manse and other houses, knocking up some furniture, making a start on the church—while the reverends got on with their preaching. But so far as he could make out, Toyne and Chuma were doing nothing. They were waiting for him to bring about all the changes. They wanted the new village with its straight streets and square houses and pumped water to come first. Smart was beginning to sense, a little obscurely, he was being asked to do something he saw no necessity for. Meanwhile, if it came to fighting, what were they fighting about?

'What will Katupha do?'

'Today, they have the funeral. Everybody there. Themba and Kuwali and everyone. They not working in the fields today. They all go funeral. Then tomorrow, they meet to decide.'

'Who?'

'All the same chiefs you see come here.'

'Then they will fight?'

'First, they will want meeting with Bwana Toyni. After, they fight.'

Smart turned abruptly and left Chuma on the path to climb back up to the village. He was going to speak with the reverend but as he reached the first huts he changed his mind and climbed past the village up Migodo hill. Since that first day with Toyne, he hadn't been up there. Even then he hadn't paid much attention to the view, being more interested in the village below. Now, he looked with more care at the ochre plain and the black conical hills. Gradually, it came to him how well chosen was the site of the village.

First, Migodo was impossible to approach from any side without being visible at least ten miles off. Any invading force could make use of the hills, but between the nearest of these and the village was a long slope without any cover at all. Even the trees had no foliage low down, spreading themselves upwards to catch the sun like inside out umbrellas. The shelf of rocky soil on which the village was actually built was approached by a steeper slope from behind. But it curved around the face of the hill with places where only three or four could pass at one time and there were several spots where it would be easy to fix an ambush.

Otherwise, any attackers would have to scramble up the paths from stream, at the mercy of whatever weapons the defenders had to hand—spears, arrows, even stones.

One thing still puzzled him. The hill was easy to defend if you had enough men. But what if the attackers simply camped by the stream and waited? Of course, as

Smart already knew, that wasn't the kind of war they fought here. Most of the fighting was over food or a slave or two and the raiders wouldn't go to the trouble of a long siege. All the same, twenty-four hours without water would be sufficient. Then he remembered. There was a trickle of water behind Themba's hut, descending the hill to the main stream. It took him more than an hour scrambling among the boulders, blackening his hands with the ash of the hot season's fires, before he found it—the sweetest, coldest of springs bubbling up from the tangled roots of a wild cashew tree. So there was water up here too. He washed his hands and drank deeply. This satisfied his sense of what was fitting, but was little to the business in hand. Migodo hill had many advantages but even with their three guns he couldn't see Toyne and himself and Chuma holding out against five-hundred attackers. That would be something more than Rorke's Drift.

But what would they be fighting over? He looked up at the black clouds gathering as they did every day towards noon.

All they needed was time, to let the season mature.

'Agnes, my dear, dear sister,' wrote Toyne as a thousand cockerels chorused outside his window, 'I need to remember always that God is our refuge and that we attempt nothing in our own name. I fear, in my human frailty, that we are building on the sand. But can it be fraud if it inspires such great faith as I have not seen, no, not in Israel?

'You will wonder that I write so, but I have seen wonders. All things work together. God plants his footsteps in the sea and rides upon the storm.

'The woman's cruel death is a deep mystery. It troubles me greatly. Chuma has told Kathupa it was a punishment for his disbelief and I have had to rebuke him. But Chuma's own faithlessness together with Banda's obedience and Smart's mechanical skills—all these were put to use in the great design.

'I had spent the night on my knees, watching and praying. I am a simple man, as you of all people understand well, and my only desire is to be of service. The chiefs had returned, as Chuma warned me they would, and I had no choice but to receive them. If you smile at my change of heart, you must reflect that after the woman's cruel death, they were coming to me on a question of faith. I was also sorely troubled about Banda. He, too, is a child of God, and in my trust.

'We met in the bwalo under the tamarind tree, we three with Chuma interpreting and Smart grunting his usual comments, and some sixty chiefs and headmen from the highlands and the lakeshore. My first words were, of course, about Banda. I told them I was meeting them in response to their request, but that nothing further could be said until I knew where Banda was or what they had done with him. They looked genuinely astonished at this and swore most solemnly they knew northing of his disappearance. Something about Chuma's translation made me suspect that the real culprit was closer to home. But more of that in a moment.

'I have to say no church assembly I ever attended was better conducted. They are courteous to a fault. Everyone turns in his seat to gaze on the face of the one who is speaking, and at the conclusion of each paragraph there is a little formula.

'"Do I speak truly?"

'"You speak truly"

'This happens even when they disagree with him. Then there is a chairman or 'speaker' who at the conclusion of every speech sums up the main points, making sure the speaker is satisfied with his summary. It sounds awfully longwinded but their speeches are very exact and precise, almost like poetry, and I think they have a tremendous respect for words. No one seems to take up unnecessary time. Chuma, of course, was translating for me, but these were my impressions. It was all very different from the bear garden of Westminster.

'Much of what they said truly amazed me. One old man called Mwale from a village twenty miles away talked for ten minutes about my snake. You recall my night visitor in the old hut? It seems it was a python, and that the visit was a great honour for me. So far as I could gather from Chuma (who is reluctant to talk of such things) they believe the python is a rain-spirit who visits the earth dressed in the colours of the rainbow. Much of the time he lives far south from here in a shrine with a human wife who utters prophecies. The gist of Chief Mwale's speech was that the meeting should take no decisions without first consulting her. Otherwise Mbona (that was the python's name) might be angry that his host (*mea culpa*) had been harmed in any way.

'Who would have thought my snake would be my protector? But there were other surprises. You will remember that before I moved to my new home I stored my Bible and prayer book in a cracked water pot to keep them safe from the rats and termites. I knew this had been misinterpreted, in the most superstitious manner, but I wasn't aware just how much they knew about my books—not only the Holy Texts but the "one where the writing stops before the edge of the page" (apparently the *Golden Treasury*) and the "one with all the pages kept secret" (I'm afraid I haven't yet cut the pages of your *Middlemarch*).

'Most worrying of all, to them, was "the book I am writing". It took me some time to realise they were describing this diary I am keeping for you. They were concerned that nothing should be put down which wasn't "true". Of course, I could reassure them about that. I don't lie to my sister, or to myself if I can help it. But that was not really what they meant. They have a fear of writing which arises from their respect for words. Spoken words can be called back if they are regretted or contradicted. But words written are written for ever. They become the truth, even if they were false, because once written they cannot be recalled. I thought at once, of course, of the opening of the fourth Gospel where "In the beginning, God" becomes "In the beginning was the Word".

'And what mimics they are! As speaker after speaker commented on all our actions since our arrival, they dropped into our very postures. One began talking of our dam and, long before Chuma could begin his translation, I could see Smart before me with his shoulders bent and his chin stuck forward and grim determination on his visage. Another of the chiefs had Chuma's hauteur to the last eyebrow. I could swear there was no disrespect in this. It was a kind of empathy, a reaching even as they spoke of us into our way of seeing.

'You will guess from this that I, too, did not escape their observation and, strange to relate (I wouldn't have believed only two days ago), I couldn't help smiling at their representation of Evensong. As I smiled, of course, they too smiled, and it turned to laughter and, after that, there could be no more talk of Kathupa's or war.

'But the problem remained as a question of faith. I promised I would meet them on the morrow and give them an answer.

'At that moment, I swear I had no intention of acting as a witchdoctor. But I felt a great love flowing from me towards them and a wish, I suppose, to gain time. So I spent the whole night on my knees, feeling the perspiration running down my spine and hoping against hope it would rain before the morrow.

'It didn't rain overnight. But dawn brought such a day of wonders as I have never encountered.

'The first surprise was Banda's safe return. He didn't announce himself and he offered no explanations. I heard noises in the kitchen which were so familiar that at first their significance eluded me. Then I sat waiting impatiently, hardly daring to believe he had returned until, yes, there he was, it was Banda serving our customary breakfast in his normal taciturn manner. Of course, I wanted to question him but before our meal was finished and I had the opportunity to get him and Chuma together, the second surprise occurred.

'There were shouts from the lower part of the village and the sound of running feet. Then a column of soldiers marched up and came to a halt in front of my house. I say "soldiers", but if I had met them anywhere in the bush I would have taken them for slavers, and I say "marched" but you never saw such an undisciplined rabble. There were a dozen of them, some black, some half-caste, with rifles and tattered uniforms, slouching in two columns, five at the front and seven at the rear.

'The officer in charge was a Portuguese, about five foot tall with a gleaming bald head and a moustache which completely veiled his mouth, as though he was talking from behind a black brush. He announced himself as Tenente Mesquita, and my first impression was that he had come to arrest us. It wasn't easy to understand him. He appeared very nervous and excitable, staring around him as though expecting danger from every side. Occasionally, he spoke the odd word in English, like "It is forbidden" or "Go back", but the rest was in nothing I recognised. In the end, we got by with Banda translating to Chuma and Chuma to me, with my answers making the same complicated journey.

'As I say, my first impression was that he had come to arrest us. He claimed this was Portuguese territory and his talk was of passports and import duties and land taxes and licenses for our firearms and building taxes and something about Geeyas and Bems and the Lord knows what else. He fired off these demands as though we were both in London, as though it was the most natural thing in the world to travel around Africa with a trunk full of official documents. I told him plainly as an Englishman I had been here for nearly three months and had seen no sign of Portuguese authority, neither on the coast nor here inland. The tattered flag his soldiers were carrying was entirely new to me. He was the first Portuguese I had met in this part of the world.

'At this, he looked very tired and depressed and began a different complaint. They had marched two days covering fifty miles without a break and were exhausted and very hungry. Even then, I had still not connected Banda's return with their arrival. But the Tenente repeated a phrase sarcastically several times, in a kind of duet with Banda, but without it featuring in Chuma's translation. It was something like *por salvar os Ingleses*, or *por salvar os Britanicos*.

'"What does he mean, salvar the English?"

'So it all tumbled out. Tenente Mesquita had come in response to a letter from Chuma, carried by Banda, stating we were in the greatest danger. At once, they had left the party of railway surveyors with whom they were serving fifty miles to the south, and had come to our rescue. I was expected to abandon our mission and return with them to the coast.

'I believe the greatest thing I did that day was to control my temper. I could not, of course, be angry with

Mesquita and his men who had gone to great trouble on our behalf. But Chuma was a different matter. Fixing him with an angry stare, I gave him my instructions.

'Mesquita and his men should be welcomed to the Mission and given our hospitality, commencing with a cooked meal. The chiefs should be told immediately that I would be conducting a prayer meeting at midday in the bwalo. The soldiers could be present if they wished, after they had rested. With that, I withdrew into my house. Chuma had plainly not expected this outcome. I was satisfied, as I turned away, to witness fear on his dusky brow.

'My dear, dear sister, you will not like these words and perhaps I deceive myself in saying I controlled my anger. There was rage in my soul, against Chuma above all others. But surely I made it serve our cause of evangelism? I recalled our beloved bishop's example in adapting our teaching to the understanding of our hearers. Truly, we attempt nothing in our own name. Moreover, my sister, my conscience, you will feel with me in my predicament. Our *Prayer Book* contains no Collects suitable for rain-making. But was I to abandon my life's work over a scruple? How many of our favourite hymns and prayers thank the Almighty for providing us with food and raiment? Is this mere poetic licence or the hand of the Lord in our good fortune?

'I sat at my table, where I am writing this, and read again with greater attention I Kings 18. As I did so, I saw my way forward, a little perhaps in the Baptist fashion, but nonetheless efficacious for that.

'At the appointed time, we assembled under the tamarind tree in the bwalo. My desk was covered with a pure white cloth on which rested my open Bible, My congregation was a thousand fold, men, women, children and babes on their mothers' arms, all seated in absolute silence behind the chiefs who squatted in a semi-circle three deep at the front. Mesquita and his men, by the bye, were standing well to the rear, with Smart in attendance at their service. I should add it was a day much like the others, oppressively hot and humid but with the black clouds building up from the coast.

'Without preamble, I began reading from the Scriptures. Chuma had the strictest instructions to translate accurately each verse word for word, without additions or threats or glosses of his own.

> *"Then Elijah said to the prophets of Baal, 'Choose for yourselves one bull and prepare it first, for you are many; then call on the name of your god, but put no fire to it.' So they took the bull that was given them, prepared it, and called on the name of Baal from morning until noon, crying, 'O Baal, answer us!' But there was no voice, and no answer. They limped about the altar that they had made. At noon Elijah mocked them, saying, 'Cry aloud! Surely he is a god; either he is meditating, or he has wandered away, or he is on a journey, or perhaps he is asleep and must be awakened."*

'I paused at this point and looked up, and began singing with Chuma and Banda the first and last verses of the hymn "O God of Bethel". It was a hymn sung at Livingstone's funeral and one which they have begun to associate with the mission. The silence was absolute. Not a soul stirred, nor so much as a baby cried. When we reached the "Amen", I at once resumed my reading.

> *"Elijah took twelve stones, according to the number of the tribes of the sons of Jacob, to whom the word of the* LORD *came, saying, 'Israel shall be your name'; with the stones he built an altar in the name of the* LORD*. Then he made a trench around the altar, large enough to contain two measures of seed. Next he*

put the wood in order, cut the bull in pieces, and laid it on the wood. He said, 'Fill four jars with water and pour it on the burnt-offering and on the wood.' Then he said, 'Do it a second time'; and they did it a second time. Again he said, 'Do it a third time'; and they did it a third time, so that the water ran all round the altar, and filled the trench also with water.

At the time of the offering of the oblation, the prophet Elijah came near and said, 'O LORD, God of Abraham, Isaac, and Israel, let it be known this day that you are God in Israel, that I am your servant, and that I have done all these things at your bidding. Answer me, O LORD, answer me, so that this people may know that you, O LORD, are God, and that you have turned their hearts back.' Then the fire of the LORD fell and consumed the burnt-offering, the wood, the stones, and the dust, and even licked up the water that was in the trench."

'It had been my intention to pause again at this point in the reading and to sing two verses of Isaac Watts' great missionary hymn "Jesus shall reign where'er the sun". But the service passed beyond my direction.

'Even as Chuma was translating the words "the fire of the Lord fell", there was a loud whooshing sound from the hillside above us and a rocket exploded high among the black clouds with stars and tumbling flares. Then another, and another, until six had gone off in rapid succession.

'I was utterly dumbfounded. I realised, of course, they were the rockets from the Albatross, but how they came to be ignited and to what purpose was a complete mystery. You will have guessed, far quicker than I did, it could only be Smart's doing. The people were on their feet and humming with fear and would have departed in panic but for two further surprises.

'First, the chiefs kept their places, looking utterly unperturbed.

'Secondly, it began to rain. It was only the lightest of drizzles but it calmed the crowd. I seized the moment and once again began reading from the Scriptures.

> *"Elijah went up to the top of Carmel; there he bowed himself down upon the earth and put his face between his knees. He said to his servant, 'Go up now, look towards the sea.' He went up and looked, and said, 'There is nothing.' Then he said, 'Go again seven times.' At the seventh time he said, 'Look, a little cloud no bigger than a person's hand is rising out of the sea.' Then he said, 'Go and say to Ahab, "Harness your chariot and go down before the rain stops you."' In a little while the heavens grew black with clouds and wind; there was heavy rain."*

'By now, it was raining steadily. Rejoicing was at hand. Yet for me, my dear sister, the greatest wonder of this day of wonders was yet to come. For when Chuma and I began singing "Praise God from whom all blessings flow", there were four women and two men who sang along with us. They remembered the hymn from twenty years back with our beloved bishop. Truly, this was a miracle. I was moved to tears.

'Do not mistake me, dear sister. I know it is Jehovah, the God of the Old Covenant, to whom I have weaned them. I know I must bring them ere long to Christ, our Blessed Saviour.

'But it is a start. Tomorrow, rain or no rain (which now, by the bye, thunders on my roof), Mesquita will return to his railway. And I shall begin planning my church.

Administering

Bangwe,
9 May, 1903

Darling Hortense,

Hurray! O Frabjous day! At last, I'm here, I'm here, in my own home and I can bathe and relax and wear clean underwear. A bit scratchy because, between you and me, Roderick's rather generous with the starch. But more of that anon.

What a journey. Do you realize how far it is to central Africa? The atlas gives you no idea you have to go round in so many circles. Like stalking an antelope, you have to get downwind of it before you can approach. And the nearer you get the more prickly and perspiring you are. Southampton to Cape Town was luxury. Cape Town to Durban perfectly pleasant. Durban to Beira, well, I'll say this for the Portuguese, they're excellent cooks and their natives are very well trained.

But then it was Beira to Chinde—or rather, off Chinde because, horribly little coaster as it was, its draught was too deep for the bar and we had to risk landing in a bumboat. I'll pause at Chinde, as we did for forty-eight hours, because what's to come is altogether too shocking for your tender ears.

Chinde's just a sandbank in the Zambesi delta. Do you remember looking at the map and how reassured we were because it was coloured red in the middle of all that yellow Portuguese coastline? All it is a sandbank, half submerged when the tide's up. The highest point's about four feet above sea level. There's a flagpole stuck in a barrel with the Union Jack hanging limp. There's a custom's house we were waved through as administration. There's what passes for a hotel, the famous Murray's, with a zinc roof to trap the heat and slow fans stirring the air like soup (if you open the windows, you are eaten alive by mosquitoes as big as turkeys).

I sat in the lounge drinking tea made with condensed milk (ugh) while Geoffrey was trying to arrange our onward passage. Apparently, Chinde's great days are over. Five years ago there was a hurricane, and the houses and the tennis court were swallowed by the sea. No ordinary tennis court. It was painted green (the concrete base, that is) with daisies and buttercups, and with honeysuckle and convolvulus climbing the net posts. The work of a subaltern, stranded here several weeks. Farewell green fields, farewell ye happy groves.

So, after this pause, are you prepared for what follows? Three days on the paddle steamer John Bowie, up the Zambesi and Shire rivers, circling and winding till my head began to spin. Then a whole day by palequin to the Highlands, and another day thereafter to Bangwe.

No, Hortense darling, let me spare you my sufferings. Suffice to say they're building a railway, so that when you come to visit me (remember your sworn oath) you'll be spared such Dante-esque torments. Suffice to mention, too, that through all this Geoffrey, despite your foreboding, proved a perfect darling. He was also, strictly *entre nous*, just a little more experienced than you anticipated.

So here I am at last, a bride in my own home in the highlands, cool and with a panoramic view of the plain and the silver, winding river. Roderick, he of the over-generous starch, is my wash boy. I have, in addition, a cook boy, a garden boy, a pot boy, a dog boy, a golf boy, and I don't know what else. I am surrounded by riches. I lack only my earliest, dearest friend. My darling, let me hear from you soon.

Your dear friend, Caroline.

P.S. 10 June. I've also got a gun boy. Heigh-Ho!

19 May, 1903

My Dearest Friend,

My last went down river to be posted at Chinde. This one's being taken by a neighbour who's going home to be posted at Cape Town, so I suppose it might arrive first. If it does, there's another on the way that will explain all.

Where has your bedfellow flown to? I live four thousand feet up, on the side of a mountain called Bangwe, looking out across the plain and the serpentine river that was our highway here. I have a bungalow with seven rooms. I have one fine, manly husband and eight very various menservants. The temperature at midday is 85°. And I am learning how to survive in such mathematical circumstances.

Did you know the moon's upside down here? Something to do with angles and refractions. I watch it sprinting through the marbled clouds coming up from the Mozambique Channel and think about how much my life has changed. I don't think I've ever been so conscious of nature before. I've always loved trees and flowers, of course, in a sort of Wordsworth manner, but I've never felt it impinged so before.

This is partly, of course, because you've got to watch out for snakes if you're strolling in your garden, and bang out your shoes each morning in case a scorpion's lodged there during the night. But it's more than that, a kind of bristling, tingling presence that refuses to remain in the background but keeps announcing itself, most of the time in shapes and colours I can't even put a name to. When I ask people for the names, they turn out to be terribly dull things like moon flower or angel's trumpet, that rob them of their awful beauty like a circus lion or a dancing bear.

I've missed my monthly visitor. I haven't told Geoffrey yet because he'll fuss too much, and in any case it's not certain. But I had to tell someone, my darling confidant. Write soon. Oh, how I wish you were here.

Your sister-in-arms, Caroline.

23 May, 1903

Dear Hortense,

This is an amazing country. It's only eleven years since the men of our administration took over and a mere four or five since wives began settling here. Yet already it's a 'society' with all the usual little secrets and jealousies and exclusions. What you were before you came here doesn't count for much. The governor used to be a big game hunter, but under him are men from Eton and Harrow

I've worked out some of the rules—it wasn't difficult (they're not very subtle) but there are some odd twists. You've got to be on the administrative side, of course. We don't talk to traders and missionaries, except at Governor's dinners. With the planters you have to be more careful. Curiously, some of them were here before the government and they reckon they're the real owners of the country. They carry a lot of weight, even when they haven't as many acres backing them as you'd expect. On the other hand, we don't talk to their managers, which is just as well since most of them seem to be Scotsmen speaking quite incomprehensible brogues.

There's no Indian Army regimental nonsense, thank God. Most of the soldiers are sepoys. But with our lot there's a pecking order, depending on your husband's post. Geoffrey's a Collector, now—no, that doesn't mean he's started collecting stamps! He's responsible for taxes and duties and runs the askari and the court for Bangwe and acts in general as political officer. Don't laugh. It's because he got promotion (he started as Acting Assistant etc) that we were able to get married at all. It's also responsible for me having this lovely house with its cool veranda and view of the plain and the river. So, you see, all this matters terribly.

If you're new to the country, and haven't yet had your first bout of fever, then everyone's entitled to patronise you—even the lowest PWD wife. But the real complications are over Africans.

I run a household with eight servants, all of them men. When Geoffrey leaves for the Boma in the morning, there I am alone with them, the wash boy, the pot boy, the garden boy, the gun boy, and so on I told you about. Did you ever hear of such a thing? I've been learning the language, so I can give my orders to the cook boy and the dog boy. At least, Geoffrey calls it learning the language. From what I've seen of African society, I don't believe there are any Nyanja words appropriate for women to give orders to men. But that's by the bye.

The thing is—remember all our arguments about Votes for Woman and the cause?—the thing to ponder is this: our men look on African women as women (Geoffrey has a dreadful colleague rumoured to have children by five African wives). But we women mustn't look at the men as men. You have to learn to treat them as eunuchs. If you fail, as a certain Mrs Currey who was caught, not by any means *en flagrante*, just sympathising over the death of a servant's child, you lose caste forever. For this is a small world of limited gossip. After all, there are only twenty-three of us.

I truly covet a letter. My monthly secret remains intact.

Your own, Caroline.

15 July, 1903

Sweetest Hortense,

Your longed-for letter arrived an hour ago by special courier (a smiling, kow-towing native in a fez), and I've read and re-read it twenty times, reclining in luxury with a gin-and-fizz on my veranda.

Yes, I've told Geoffrey. He's full of surprises. He was pleased, of course. Don't ever doubt that. But instead of being irritatingly attentive, making me lie down while he crooned his affection, denying me any right to move a limb, he just gave a quick smile and behaved like any experienced administrator faced with a difficulty he had entirely foreseen. As you see, I'm in good hands.

Actually, he's away this week on ulendo—a sort of tour of inspection he makes once a month, choosing a different part of the district each time. He goes from village to village, talking with the chiefs and elders, checking the taxes and hearing cases and generally informing himself about what's going on. He promised to take me with him, but he goes by bicycle and the bush tracks are a bit bumpy for a woman in my condition. As for the palaquin that is the other option. No thanks. Not after my experience coming up here from the river.

Do you know what his job was when he first came here? He spent most of the time in the office at Kathupa's (that's up country, by the lake) granting divorces. I couldn't believe it when he told me, strait-laced Geoffrey of all people.

There's a tribe that migrated here in the middle of last century, loosely connected with the Zulus about whom we used to hear so much. Before they came, the custom was for men, when they got married, to go and live in their wives' villages. Everything was done through the woman's line so that, for instance, a man had no control over his children who were regarded as actually 'belonging' to the wife and her brothers. Then, when the more-or-less Zulus came, everything changed. The women married into the men's households and became the men's property, rather like us until a few years back.

The joke is that when we came here (i.e., the Governor and Geoffrey and all the others), we actually agreed with the what's-it-Zulus about how to run a household. But we were also here, so we said, to do away with the slave trade, and the women regarded this type of marriage as slavery. Geoffrey had a queue outside his office every morning of women wanting to be free. So he gave them their divorces, much to the disgust, he says, of his messenger boy Kuwali who, as a Muslim, thought all these waiting women were thoroughly immoral.

It makes you think. Tell me, darling Hortense, was there a time in our distant ancestry when everything was in the female line? Isn't it more natural, if you consider it? Anyway, what resulted here, according to Geoffrey, was that the divorced women built new villages in the bush beyond anybody's control, and collecting taxes was impossible. So the policy was changed. Isn't that sad?

All the same, I can't see you and me flocking off from Ludlow into the Welsh hills and founding a new village. And why on earth should I want to, in my 'interesting condition'.

Your tale about Isabel had me in stitches. Will she ever settle for what's to hand? Yet she makes me yearn. Bill the farmer and Bob the trader and Ben the bank manager are such limited options. Perhaps she should come out here. We have on offer the empire builder, the strong, silent type, not the greatest of conversationalists, but a man to depend on (so I trust).

Don't take this too seriously. He's away, and I'm temporarily abandoned to my thoughts, except for your dearest letter.

Your ever faithful, Caroline.

23 August, 1903

Faithful Hortense,

I've found a new friend. Gosh, that sounds terribly melodramatic. I mean someone at last I can talk to, without minding all the mindless rules.

I had some slight pains last week. Geoffrey was in court all day, and I panicked rather and dashed off to the hospital at the Scottish Mission. The sister there is called Agnes Littlejohn and she turns out to be from Leominster. Do you remember the corn merchant in the main square? That's the family—she's a cousin of the chap with his name over the shop doorway. I learned this while she was giving me a thorough check-up, and pronounced me guilty of nothing worse than indigestion.

Afterwards, she showed me the delivery room and I met the nurse in charge, an African lady called Charity. We three sat down together and had a cup of tea, and suddenly I realised this was the first time I'd had a proper conversation with an African. Of course, she 'Mrs Clunies-Rowland-ed' (or rather she named me Mrs

Crunies-Lowland) while I called her Charity, so we weren't just women together. But, do you know, Hortense, she was intelligent and good-humoured, and talked about her children just as any of us would have done. She told me about some of the customs they are trying to discourage, like letting your grandmother stand on your stomach to encourage delivery. I found myself envying Sister Agnes, for being so much closer to the people here than any of us can manage up at the station.

Though I suppose she's only doing what Geoffrey does most days, and it's us wives who cut ourselves off. But there's another difference. Geoffrey's dealing with chiefs and the old ways, trying to administer their customs. The missionaries are trying to change things, by educating people. I haven't made up my own mind what I think about this, but I do admire Agnes (for we've become friends) for living on a kind of dangerous border between what's good and what's bad in their ways and in ours. After all, don't we want women to be making their own decisions?

I told Geoffrey I was adding Agnes to the list of 'people we talk to'. He pulled a bit of a face at this, because he thinks missions are a nuisance. 'What are all these educated natives going to do?' he asks, and I must admit I don't know the answer. But once he'd met her, and she told him roundly, 'One day, they're going to replace you' and there were no further problems. I think Geoffrey secretly admires independent-minded women.

The railway makes progress, and not just on paper. It's become connected in my mind with the prospect of seeing you here, and showing you our 'society' and our upside down moon.

Your loving Caroline (Crunies-Lowland)

6 September, 1903

Hortense my dearest,

This is a dramatic season. The cold has gone—you'd be surprised how cold it was up here in the Highlands. We had fires every night and one morning in early August I swear there was frost on the plateau overlooking the town.

It's getting warmer, but Agnes says it's too soon for the rains. At night the skies are cloudless, but we have tremendous electrical storms, great trees of forked lightning criss-crossing the black dome between the mountain and the plain, bequeathing in their wake absolute darkness—Milton's 'darkness visible'—stars and moon obliterated, until our eyesight recovers before the next explosion.

Every time it happens I can feel a little jump in my belly, as though my baby is wired to the telegraph. It makes me dream of revolutions and utopia.

I went to the market yesterday in a village just below the boma. Agnes had told me about it, and when I arrived there and was feeling a little lost, who popped up out nowhere but nurse Charity? I suppose actually it's only because of her that Agnes knows about it, but at the time it seemed a providential coincidence.

It was all so interesting, a tremendous ferment of activity, so much haggling, so much chattering, so many incomprehensible things for barter (or for sale, there's money here now) being proclaimed while hundreds of men and women milled and circled in a manner a bit like an electrical storm. It made me feel, what on earth are we doing, Geoffrey and the missionaries, when there is so much they are able to do for themselves?

Charity showed me some of the different vegetables, and I came home with a basket full of roots and greens with incomprehensible names. The joke is when I showed them to Salazar (my cook boy), he didn't know how to prepare them. He only knows white man's 'relish', he said. His wife would laugh at him if he cooked the vegetables I had brought. So I ended up by throwing them away. But I'm not going to be beaten by this. Next market day, I'm going to try again.

Meanwhile, I thought I'd try something else and went down to the lines to talk to some of our servants' wives. It wasn't a success. I wanted to be friendly, but it was too much like Lady Bountiful visiting the peasants. At first they were frightened and all scampered indoors to change their clothes, leaving their cooking pots simmering with all sorts of strange smells. I tried to sort out who was whose wife and eventually made some progress. But I only know how to give orders in their language, and I couldn't keep the dismay out of my face at how they have to live.

Really, the servants' lines are an affront—bleak rows of brick huts with tin roofs and damp concrete floors. People keep saying it's better than they have in their villages, but I don't believe it. Nor, by the bye, does Geoffrey, who sometimes actually stays in the villages when he's on ulendo.

You can see as well as finding friends, I'm finding work to do.

Your loyal Caroline.

P.S. Some of the wives aren't happy with me. I mean our twenty-three aristocats. What larks.

1 November, 1903

Dearest Hortense,

Something rather serious has happened and I must write it out, with you in mind. Oh dear, I'm sorry, don't worry, we're all fine. I'm sorry, too, for the long gap between letters. I'm seven months now and becoming high, but it's all been feeling much better since the morning sickness stopped.

Let me begin with how I found out. Geoffrey's away on ulendo again, the long one that takes ten days. On Thursday, Roderick came to tell me an old man wanted to speak with me. I found him waiting by the veranda steps, wearing an old jacket I thought I'd seen before somewhere, and twisting his hat in his hands. So I got him up and sat down—he refused to sit himself—while he told me he was likoswe and that the child was very sick, and that he'd come to see the bwana because he was frightened about the child. It took a long time to sort all this out and I didn't know what likoswe was (I just assumed he was some kind of chief). But anyway, there was a sick child, so I told Roderick to take them to the hospital and gave him a note and said to be sure to see Sister Agnes.

On Friday, I popped in at the hospital just to say hello, and we chatted as usual. I asked about the old man and the child—at that stage, I didn't even know whether it was a boy or a girl—and Agnes said the boy had a fever but I needn't worry because it wasn't serious and he could go home in a few days.

It was on my way home I thought there was something strange about all this. I stopped and sat down—there's a bench under the jacarandas near the old boma—and when I'd thought for a bit I went back to see Agnes again.

'What's a likoswe?' I asked.

'It's a relative,' she told me, 'usually an uncle, who takes responsibility for arranging a woman's marriage. Then afterwards, for dealing with any problems that arise.'

'But why should this likoswe come to me?'

At this, Agnes looked panic-stricken.

'You mean, you don't know?' she said. 'Oh dear Lord, when you sent the boy to me, I assumed you already knew.'

Well, of course, by that stage, the penny had begun to drop.

The boy is Geoffrey's. I went to the ward to look at him and there could never have been any doubt. A lovely, brown eight-year-old, fast asleep, with his father's forehead and brown eyes and a flat nose and tight reddish curls.

'I thought you knew,' Agnes said again.

'Do you know the mother?'

'I only know he's your husband's boy.'

Hortense, dearest, you mustn't imagine I'm stupidly jealous. What Geoffrey did before I met him is his own business, and I know full well I don't have any rivals. But there's the child. What's to be done about him? And, before that, there's the coupling. What's to be said about that?

It's not the end of the world. That's what you would tell me, I suppose, though by the time you get this letter the world may well be trembling somewhat. Geoffrey gets back in three days and we shall have to it out. I must admit, I do think he should have told me. After all, in the end, my truest friend, it's a question of friendship.

Your very own, Caroline.

P.S. 5 November. There's been no one going down river so I've re-opened this today. Geoffrey returned from ulendo two nights ago. It's all worse than I thought. There are four of them, three boys and a girl, by three women in different villages. Oh, dearest Hortense, what in heaven's name am I going to do?

11 December, 1903

Dear Miss Leadbetter,

My wife has asked me to write to announce the birth of our son Harold Geoffrey on 9 December at the Mission hospital here in Bangwe. She and Harold are both well. The baby weighed 7lbs 10 oz.

She thanks you warmly for your recent letters, which she says have given her much support, and she promises to write as soon as she leaves the hospital. These have been anxious weeks for both of us, and we all rejoice at her safe delivery.

With kind regards.
Yours sincerely,
Geoffrey Clunies-Rowland.

2 February, 1904

Dear Hortense,

I'm so sorry for my long neglect of you. Your letters have been a great comfort, though at times Isabel's predicaments and even your own campaigning have all seemed a very long way off. In hospital, I felt I was drifting days at a time down a winding green river with many different channels, unable to see beyond the plumed reeds and exploding heads of papyrus on either side.

Then I came home with Harold and, of course, had to pull myself together. He's a tough little fellow and very demanding. Sometimes I can't believe he's mine, but he's got my brow and nose and I think his eyes will be grey-green eventually (his chin's definitely Geoffrey's). I've got a lovely nursemaid called Emily to help out—one of Charity's little nieces she's loaned me on condition I help improve her English. It works both ways because at last I'm learning some proper Nyanja instead of just the madam variety.

What I couldn't understand—one of the many things I couldn't get clear—was why I was the one to blame in all this. What 'happened' was just one of many things that happened before the wives came out here. I'm at fault, they say, not Geoffrey, for prying into what's best forgotten. As for the children, they're a betrayal of everything we're here to represent. To draw attention to them is unpardonable. Even Agnes seems to think, as she puts it, least said soonest mended.

For the moment, I'm just recovering my strength and looking after Harold, and not thinking ahead too much. Please keep writing, despite my silences.

Your friend, Caroline.

15 February, 1904

Dear Hortense,

I feel a little odd defending Geoffrey to you, but one of your letters last year was so angry with him, I can't just leave it at that and say nothing. I know you're writing out of your love for me and I'm eternally grateful. But 'for better or worse' I've joined my life to his, and I can't just give up at the first hurdle.

The truth is, I've been in a muddle. What is it I accuse him of? Of behaving like an animal? That's what the station thinks, and chooses to turn a blind eye to—on the grounds it happened before the wives arrived to set some proper standards.

He told me how it all started with Peter's mother (Peter's the eight-year-old who had the fever). She was one of the women he allowed to divorce. Asawilunda's her name, and he remembered her when he met her again on ulendo. What struck me, as he was talking, was that he looked on her a person, something the station wives refuse to do.

Can you imagine it? He used to lock up the office on Friday afternoon, and cycle the sandy footpaths to her village, with the District Book in the saddle bag to work on over the weekend, and then cycle back on Monday morning. He kept this up for four years, until he was transferred from Kathupa's to Bangwe, after which he saw her and the baby only occasionally. The point is, it was a happy time, a kind of idyll which he knew was only temporary. In a curious way, it's because he's capable of doing something like this that I love him.

Of course, that doesn't account for the others. About them, he just says that on ulendo in the old days, sometimes the chief would give you not just a hut but a woman to look after you, which certainly isn't very romantic but it was in the culture—and in any case, it's all water under the bridge.

Except, of course, for the children. I find that's my sticking point—that I can't just ignore them as I'm supposed to. There's Peter and his sister Maria who's five. There's Paul, who's four, and little Daniel who'll be one next month. Apparently (to our eternal shame), all these half-breed children have Bible names, but they can't be legally registered because our Great Empire on which the sun never sets won't recognise they officially exist. What makes it worse is that London has issued a couple of official circulars on 'Concubinage with Native Women'. They're not retroactive, of course, no problem there. But the children are the living evidence. To mention them seems like flouting the new rules.

I still feel he should have told me about them, not let me be ambushed like this. He asked if he'd told me, would I have married him? Would I? I don't know. Because if he'd told me back in Shropshire, it would have been before I knew Bangwe and the twenty-three wives, before I'd met Charity and before I had set eyes on Peter and seen Geoffrey in his little features.

Don't worry about me, Hortense, I'm slowly getting back on my feet, I promise you. Oh, I forgot to thank you for Harold's little jacket. It'll start getting chilly again at nights in about two month's time and will be perfect for him then.

My love, Caroline.

1 March, 1904

In haste, Hortense, (the messenger boy's waiting)

I've sent you a small tin trunk containing two locally-carved folding chairs. One's for you, the other's for Isabel's wedding. With luck, they'll arrive in time. I want you to have first choice and give the other one to her.

Don't make up your mind too quickly. The one I like best has six interlocking people, all carved from a single piece of ebony. The other has a lion's head and four paws as legs. At first glance, it seems more impressive. I don't insist you give that one to Isabel but I think in the end you'll prefer the message of the first. Neither of them is actually for sitting on, unless you're more upholstered than I remember.

My love to you both, Caroline.

8 May, 1904

My most faithful friend,

Hortense, it's a whole year since I arrived. It seems an odder year than anything in Lewis Carroll.

I've much to tell you. First, Peter and Paul are going to school in Beira. It's run by the Misericordia, a Roman Catholic charity. Yes I know we're CofE Hortense, but you've no idea how many bridges I've had to cross. In British Africa there's no provision for boys like these. On the Portuguese side, there are thousands of them and, more importantly, they exist in the official mind. Maria we're sending home to England, to stay with Geoffrey's mother in Ludlow, until we ourselves return or she's grown up, whichever happens first. As for Daniel, he stays with his mother, until he's old enough to join his brothers in Beira.

All this was an immense labour, though in the end it was one of love. Geoffrey accepted my ultimatum, and it remained only to speak with his 'wives'. A year ago, I'd never dreamt I'd end up a Muslim, but they're allowed four wives and I find I've become the fourth. What a fate for a suffragette.

Charity was the key to all this. How marvellous that her name should speak out so. It turns out her elder sister married an artisan called Smart attached to the original Migode mission, so she understands the problems of such children.

I travelled with her to Kathupa's and we met Asawilunda. It was very strange to talk to a woman my husband had loved and yet who was never a rival. She was no beauty, just a solid, immensely calm presence. She was glad to meet me, and glad I had plans for Peter and Maria, those white children whose future worried her. For you see, although we are in the habit of thinking them theirs, they are in the habit of calling them white.

She had another reason for being content I didn't entirely understand. Somehow or other, her grandmother's death by lightning was associated with the first mission. Whatever this was, it made her well-disposed towards my plans for her children. She has a son by another marriage, and was glad to learn I was similarly blessed.

Paul was more of a problem. Charity had to pay her for the child which put me awkwardly in mind of the slave trade. As for why Geoffrey liked the woman—well, he must have been very tired from his journey and the night (enough said) a dark one. As for Daniel who's just a toddler, he'll stay with his mother for the time being.

Hortense, I rely on you to help out with Maria. After school, she will need connections. Geoffrey prospers, threatening to circumvent the obstacle of an unsuitable wife. Harold's greedier than ever, the little *man*!

Your own, Caroline

Ulendo

There was a chief who had two sons. The elder was by his second wife, the younger by his first wife. After his first wife proved barren, he took her sister as chimbiri wife. And then came the sons. So his household was a riddle, and was never at peace.

When the time came, the elder son went to work Ku-Joni. He walked to Beira, the new Portuguese city, and afterwards took the steamer to Lourenço Marques, and then the train to the gold mines.

Oh, there are ladders going down
Mama,
Oh, there are ladders going down
Baba,
Where will I get the courage
to step in the cage?
Oh, there are ladders going down
Mama,
Oh, there are ladders going down
Baba,
Where will I get the courage
to step in the cage?

After two years he came home, with a blanket and a radio, and his mother made a great feast. He had a card from WENELA with six moons on the back. When he had counted six moons, it was time to go back.

After four years, he came home with money to pay lobola. His father found him a wife, and he went back again ku-Joni, and he left her pregnant and cultivating his garden.

Meanwhile, the younger son was still herding his father's goats. When his time came, it was war and he went to the barracks to enlist in the Kings African Rifles. First, he travelled to Tanganyika to fight the Germani, the men with the helmets.

A ulendo,
a ulendo,
The journey,
the journey,
Change gear, driver,
hurry!
Change gear, driver,
for the men of war.
A ulendo,
a ulendo,
The journey,
the journey,

He was away for two years. He travelled to Northern Rhodesia and Kenya and Mozambique, which was a life of suffering. His mother grieved because he was lost. He saw white people killing each other. Then he came home, and his mother found out that he had lost part of his leg. Because of this, the government paid him £10, £5 for his discharge and £5 for his leg.

Nobody had ever heard of so much money. Part of it he used to buy tools to become a carver of wood. The second part he used to buy a mature ebony tree. Then he sat down and carved himself a new leg, and used the third part of the money to pay lobola to get married like his brother.

When his elder brother heard of his good fortune, he was full of hatred. He saw that after all these years, and in spite of being the elder he was going to be supplanted in the homestead. He said to his mother, 'What shall I do?' and his mother said, 'You must kill your brother. But you must make it look as if a thief did it.'

That night, he crept into the younger brother's hut. But when he lifted his spear to stab his brother, the ebony leg jumped up and sang:

Dance, leg,
You must dance alone,
Far from where you left your brother.

And the leg began beating the elder brother about the buttocks, so that he ran away into the night.

'What shall I do?' he asked his mother, and his mother said, 'You must kill your brother. But you must make it look as if an animal did it.'

Next morning, he dressed in a baboon skin, and when his younger brother went to inspect his wife's work in the garden, he attacked him. But the ebony leg jumped up and sang:

Dance, leg,
You must dance alone,
Far from where you left your brother.

And the leg began beating the elder brother about the shoulders, so that he ran away into the bush.

'What shall I do?' he asked his mother, and his mother said, 'You must kill your brother. But you must make it look as if his wife did it.' And she gave him a poison mixed from herbs.

That evening, as he walked through the courtyard, he lifted the lid of the cooking pot and he added the herbs. But the ebony leg jumped up and sang:

Dance, leg,
You must dance alone,
Far from where you left your brother.

And the leg began beating the elder brother and his mother about the head, so that they ran down to the bank of the river, and there they both drowned.

So Mavuso became the greatest carver in the land, and even the white people came to buy his carvings.

Flags

I was a boy, herding goats, not yet circumcised when the flags came. Chief Chikunda had a Union Jack on a tall pole, with ropes for pulling it up and down. Village headman Chiwewe, whose second wife ran off to live with Chikunda, had the flag of the Portuguese. It was a joke that headman Chief Mavuso kept both flags in a sack, waiting for which way the winds would blow.

For a long time it was all just a joke. Then one day, Portuguese soldiers came, looking for workers to build the new road from Mocuba. The work was without pay so no one wanted to go with the soldiers. Everyone in Chiwewe's village ran across the border, and the cypais stopped when they saw the English flag. Soon afterwards, the sepoys of the English came to Chikunda's collecting hut tax. The people away to Chiwewe's, and again they stopped. So we understood somewhere on the path between Chikunda's and Chiwewe's there was a line. But however hard we looked we couldn't see anything.

Afterwards, it became more difficult to run away. The English and the Portuguese helped each other and, if you didn't have the right documents for where you were, you were arrested and sent to work anyway. But we found out other things. Karim opened a store in Chikunda's. He wanted to trade in wild rubber, groundnuts and sesame, and if you had enough to sell he paid you in silver rupees. He sold iron hoes and calico and black biriwita cloth, and they were cheaper than in Mocuba because the English taxes were lower. But then Abdul Hassim opened another store in Chiwewe's. He paid for our oil seeds with salt and cloth and, when we complained, he said the Portuguese made him do this. But some people preferred it this way, because they were nervous about money, and when Hassim put a Swahili boy on the veranda with a sewing machine to put hems on the cloth, most of the women preferred to deal with him.

So you see, when I was growing up I already had to think about where I wanted to be, something my grandfather never had to worry about. If he moved his village it was because he was running away from the slavers, not because he had choices. After I was circumcised, a lot of our people ran away again to the English side because the Portuguese began their own form of slavery. People had to work for them for part of the year in the sisal plantations near the coast. Everybody hated this, because to walk there was dangerous, with lions on the road, and because sisal leaves are very painful to handle. But I didn't run away with them because the Scottish missionaries made a school on the Portuguese side just ten miles from Chiwewe's, and I went there, and it was there I learned to write in English. The Portuguese didn't like it, and after Mr Truscot was killed in the war with the Germans they closed it down.

Another thing I had to think about was what to call myself. My father was called Kwiri, son of Chimilengo. It is not the custom for me to reveal my navel name, but at my circumcision I was given the name Mafambisse, which is a name my people brought back from the sisal plantations, not one of our names at all. It means 'Walker', and it meant I would be a traveller, which has been true.

Then, at the Scottish school, I was given the name Smart. They told me this was the name of 'a great servant of Africa'. These words puzzled me because I didn't know white men could be servants. Afterwards, I came to understand it was just their way of saying he died in Africa after living here for a long time. When I met his daughter, a brown lady living in Mpea, down on the Zambesi, she showed me a photograph of him taken when he was in his coffin. He had fallen from the scaffolding of the new cathedral he was building in the capital. I couldn't see much of him, except that he was white, which was all she really wanted to show me.

But Smart wasn't a name to get a job with. Whenever I went to a labour office and said I was Smart, they pulled a face at me and hoped I wasn't smart-arse or smart Alec, and even when they'd made their little joke they were reluctant to take me on. So I became Aleki instead, just so that I could laugh back at them, and Aleki's what I became.

So you see again, even the names involved choices.

There was no point in saying any of this to the Commission of Enquiry 1917. All they wanted was:

Name: Aleki Smart
Date of birth: 18 June 1884
How do you know? The missionaries told me when I went to school.
Place of birth: (naturally, I chose) Mavuso's
Tribe: Achikunda.

They talked like people who hadn't brought names and flags and borders and tribes to Africa.

Oh, and my English? It's smart, damn smart, to remember to talk like a native.

*

Commission of Enquiry into the Native Rebellion of August 1917.

53rd day

Archbishop Toyne
Mr Clunies-Rowland
Mr Donald MacDonald
Mr Bruce Barrow
Mr Henry Bingham QC

Mr Aleki Smart, witness.

Chairman: Now then, Smart, I've been reading the transcript—
Bingham: Excuse me, Mr Chairman.
Chairman: Yes, Mr Bingham?
Bingham: I think Mr Smart, don't you?
Chairman: Quite right, Mr Bingham. Mister Smart, I've been reading the record concerning you. You were arrested at the Malosa border on the morning of 17th August, crossing from Portuguese East. You were detained for two months at Mpatamanga prison while charges were prepared against you. On October 23rd, you were formally charged with complicity in the Native rebellion. At your trial, you produced written testimony from your employer, Namagoa Sisal, to the effect that on the three days in question you were in attendance at the company's Ingode Compound performing your employer's business. On the strength of this evidence, you were formally acquitted by Judge Goddard, and have since resumed your duties with Namagoa Sisal. Is that correct?
Smart: Nearly, sir.
Chairman: Nearly, sir? Have the goodness to explain to me where I may be mistaken.

Smart: Namagoa Sisal sacked me, sir. Because I was arrested.
Chairman: But it was they got you acquitted.
Smart: Yes, sir. But they don't like to be involved. Not before, not after, sir. So they tell me to take my posho and go.
Chairman: Well, of course, that's none of our business, Mr Smart. However, for the purposes of the present enquiry, I think it would be helpful if you could explain a little more about the nature of your activities in Portuguese Africa. I'm sure you are aware that many of the rebels were immigrants from that side, and that when—
Bingham: If I may, Mr Chairman.
Chairman: Certainly, Mr Bingham.
Bingham: I suggest the witness should be advised of two things. First, that this is not a trial but a public enquiry intended to ascertain certain facts. Secondly, that under British law no man may be tried twice for the same offence. However, given that Mr Smart may be reasonably apprehensive lest his testimony result in fresh charges, I should like him to have your assurance, as Chairman of this Commission of Enquiry, that no prosecutions will follow from anything he tells us today. Given Mr Smart's expert knowledge of the background to this very sorry affair, I should like the enquiry to have the full benefit of that knowledge.
Chairman: If you think it's really necessary, Mr Bingham.
Bingham: Let the record show that, as a witness volunteering evidence to this enquiry, Mr Smart is granted immunity from any prosecution which may arise from that evidence.
Chairman: Is all that clear to you, Smart, Mr Smart?
Smart: Yes, sir, except—
Chairman: What now?

Smart: I don't know who this gentleman is. I remember who you are, sir, when you were Reverend Toyni in Migodo and I was a little boy. I remember Bwana Lowland before he went to work for Mr Rhodes' company. I know Mr Barrow because his land is next to mine and we have had a case over the boundary markers. And I have read Mr MacDonald's history about how the slave trade ended. But this gentleman I have not been introduced to.

Chairman: Mr Henry Bingham is a Queen's Councillor from London, representing, well, representing—

Bingham: Representing due procedure, Mr Chairman.

Chairman: Just so. Exactly. But one moment, Mr Smart. You say you knew me in Migodo. Are you connected in any way with Thomas Smart?

Smart: The Scottish school give me his name, sir. And I met his daughter.

Bingham: Who is this person, Mr Chairman?

Chairman: It's not for the record. He was an artisan who once worked for Migodo mission. Then he went native. Took an African wife. I'm surprised the Presbyterians legalised the arrangement.

Mr Clunies-Rowland: Hm! Perhaps we could proceed, Mr Chairman.

Chairman: Certainly, Mr Rowland. Now Mr Smart, it would help us if you would tell us something about your activities at Namagoa Sisal. Your former activities, that is.

Smart: I did work in the Labour Office, sir. With the boys from Central Africa. It start with Mr Pontin, when he was resident at Bangwe. He was collecting boys to go and work Portuguese side. The company tell him they go pay Hut Tax for every boy he recruit, and five shilling bonus. The boys work for six month, and the company send him the wages so he pay them when they come home.

Macdonald: You mean that while Mr Pontin was employed as a government official, he was also recruiting labour for a company in Portuguese Africa?
Smart: It was to pay Hut Tax, sir. That time, people were paying in millet because the work here was too little.
Mr Clunies-Rowland: This was quite normal at the time, Mr MacDonald.
Smart: Mr Pontin need someone to take the boys to Namagoa, so I walk with them and deliver them. When I arrive, I find the pay very good that side. Here, I get three shilling a month. Portuguese side, an educated native make ten shilling. I speak English and Portuguese and Nyanja and Yao. I write good English. Not many mistakes. So I stay and get good money.
Chairman: Are there other boys from here working that side?
Smart: Yes, sir. On the railway. In the port. On the sugar estates. I have good friends, all making the same ten shilling.
Bingham: As a class, are these natives you speak of hostile to British rule?
Smart: No sir, people say they are very well off here, better than in adjoining countries. As always, a thing has its advantages and disadvantages as well, but I might try to set out the advantages because a native under the British flag obtains what I might call 'a benefit to every class of people'. The abolition of slavery is the first point they begin with to praise the government. The free travelling of any native or stranger to and fro could not happen without the country being at peace. There is the introduction of goods and helpful things of every description a person can relate. Salt is no longer cooked in the mud at Lake Shirwa. Fire is kindled without sticks rubbing against each other. No native blacksmith is trying his best at making those blunt, shapeless hoes and axes.

No tiresome journeys are undertaken to the coast after clothing, and not a single person sits on the huge log with a wooden cross-marked hammer trying to make bark cloth. I would specifically praise the free education we have received and obtained, which makes it possible to go to look for better work.

Chairman: Yet you prefer to work in Portuguese East?

Smart: That is where I find the better work. Until now.

Chairman: Now, tell us Smart, Mr Smart, what were you actually doing on August 10th?

Smart: It is four years now I am in charge of the compound at Ingode.

Chairman: What compound is that? That's not at Namacura Sisal, is it?

Smart: No, sir, at Ingode. After I work for Mr Pontin, walking with the boys to Portuguese side, I get job with the labour office. Then the Portuguese make new rules. No one walking to work must walk too far. There have to be compounds for them to stay one night before they walk on next day. I look after the compound at Ingode. Twenty-three huts, six men each hut. When the boys arrive, I tell them where to sleep, where to cook food. I keep register. If they are journeying to work, I give them a ganyão. Sometimes, they buy food from me. I have a piece of farm there, and my wife keeps chicken and casava.

Bingham: What is ganyão, please?

Mr Clunies-Rowland: It's an advance on wages. Once accepted, they are legally bound to that employer.

Smart: Yes, sir. Otherwise, there come men from the sugar estates, coconut plantations, coffee and tea and cotton and the railway, all trying to steal the boys.

Barrow: Do I understand you correctly? Namagoa Sisal pays you ten shillings a month to manage this transit compound?

Smart: Yes, sir.
Barrow: They also entrust you with money for the boys' ganyão?
Smart: Yes, sir. I have to keep register, with full accounting.
Barrow: But you also have land there—how much land is this?
Smart: It twenty hectares, sir. But it not my land. I rent it from the company for three shilling.
Barrow: You grow food on this land, or your wife does. How many wives have you got?
Smart: One wife, sir. The other one here in Bangwe.
Barrow: You wife in Ingode grows food which you sell to the boys and they pay with their ganyão?
Smart: It depend, sir. The boys not there all the time. Sometimes it better to sell to the company. Or to Ibrahim from Quelimane. These days, it best to sell to the army.
MacDonald: Christianity and Commerce, Mr Barrow. Christianity and Commerce!
Mr Clunies-Rowland: How big is your estate in Bangwe?
Smart: Not an estate, sir. Just eight hectares. But it's my land, properly paid for and properly surveyed.
Barrow: That's a matter of opinion.
Chairman: What's that?
Barrow: Nothing to the purpose, Mr Chairman.
MacDonald: What crops do you grow in Bangwe?
Smart: I grow food, sir. And I grow tobacco. I believe African-grown tobacco could be very big in this country.
Barrow: You see, gentlemen. This is just the sort of thing that will stop this colony ever becoming rich.
MacDonald: What can you possibly mean by that?
Barrow: I don't deny Mr Smart has a sharp eye for a business proposition. But when the native is taught to work, not just to grow food but to produce exportable commodities, that's when this colony will prosper. In

Rhodesia, natives are forbidden to grow tobacco and the prosperity of that country is plain to see. What Mr Smart proposes will be the ruin of us.
MacDonald: Unfortunately, Mr Barrow, or fortunately as the case me be, that is the nub of the problem. Central Africa is a protectorate, not a colony. The interests of the natives are paramount.
Barrow: That may be very moral. But this is an agricultural country. There's simply no place here for educated natives.
Chairman: Gentlemen, please! I suggest we take a brief recess.

Not in front of the natives. Are you impressed by their questions? By the cutting edge of their forensic skill? Why shouldn't I be sarcastic? Have you understood yet what they wanted from me?

I don't think they knew themselves. They'd had the fright of their lives, four planters killed in one night and the rest of the colony in a panic. Yet they understood so little about it, they don't even know how lucky they were it wasn't all much worse. There were rebellions on the Portuguese side too. If we Africans had combined together, we could have—well, I don't know what. Those flags had made a difference. We didn't want the past back, but we'd no vision of any future. Certainly, Ebenezer Chibambo had no idea where he was heading. My own belief is he simply wanted martyrdom. That's not a river I'm willing to follow.

They'd had the fright of their lives. But who were they to blame? Ebenezer was a Christian. Brought up, like me, in the Scottish Mission. It was as though David Livingstone's own godson had raised his hand against them. Which was Mr MacDonald's view of things. He'd like to get rid of the likes of Mr Barrow and run the whole colony as a kind of presbytery. I'd like to get rid of Mr Barrow, too, but that's because he keeps trying to steal my land. The river makes a curve and gives me a nice dambo garden he'd like to get his hands on.

So Barrow wants rid of Africans like me. He prefers to deal with 'raw natives'—that's what he calls those who haven't been to school. He calls me 'half-baked'. Sometimes, really, the pain makes you laugh. And he likes to deal with chiefs. The chiefs are Muslims, and he likes that too. He calls them gentlemen—keep us Christians in our place. His problem is he can't rely on his Muslims either. On the Portuguese side, they were the ones fighting with the Germans, and it was Mr Truscot from the Scottish Mission who was killed. Right there, poor man, before my eyes.

So who was to blame? Everybody, their Christians, their Muslims, their 'raw natives' seemed to be against them. As for Reverend Toyni, ever since he came to Africa he's been looking for a government he could deal with. Temporal power, spiritual power. So he ends up working with Bwana Clunies-Rowland. And all he was ever concerned with was the company and his budget. He'd be very happy if he could just say it all started on the Portuguese side. That's what he wants me to tell him.

Was I complicit in the rising? Of course, I was. Of course, I wasn't. It's a stupid question. I knew Ebenezer Chibambo. He was my friend. We were at school together, Portuguese side, before he went to America. We both knew about the flags. When he built his church, sometimes I went there to hear him preach. He was famous because he was the first to say straight out and plain. This country is not about abolishing the slave trade. This country is about stealing our land.

What these white people don't understand is this. We are not 'faithful' or 'dangerous'. When we said 'Wait and see' we wanted to know where Ebenezer was taking us. When we say 'Yes bwana, no bwana' we're just keeping all our options open.

Commission of Enquiry into the Native Rebellion of August 1917

53rd day (resumed)

Chairman: Let me take you back, Smart, Mr Smart, to your earlier testimony when you said there were advantages and disadvantages about British rule.
Smart: Yes, sir.
Chairman: Tell us about these so-called disadvantages.
Smart: Mr Barrow say the colony is agricultural. It is true, God has not given us gold mines. For that we have to go ku-Joni, to Johannesburg. But we Africans know our land. We know how to grow millet and maize and chick-pea and cassava, a hundred things. We know the soils, and what grows best here and what grows best there, and what grows best together and what we have to grow apart. How you think we did live here, hundreds and hundreds of years, before David Livingstone come?
Chairman: You were being sold as slaves.
Smart: It is true. That is the first big advantage. There is peace in the land. But the colony is agricultural and the white man will not let us grow things.
Chairman: No one stops you growing things.
Smart: If I work for Mr Barrow, I earn money and I pay three shilling tax. If I work for myself and earn money, I have to pay six shilling tax. That is big disadvantage.
MacDonald: Let me be clear on this. The law says if you work for a European, you pay three shillings.

Smart: Yes, sir.
MacDonald: But if you work on your own account?
Smart: Six shilling, sir.
MacDonald: What happens if you go to work in Portuguese East?
Smart: Six shilling, sir. And poll tax for my wife that side.
Mr Clunies-Rowland: All this is well known, Mr MacDonald. The colony needs labour.
Smart: Yes, sir. Because white people own the land. That is biggest disadvantage. That is disadvantage every native complains of. We know this land, but we can't farm because ignorant white people have taken it.
Chairman: Be careful of your language, Smart.
Bingham: Let Mr Smart speak.
Smart: I am very sorry, sir. I am not a rebel. I do not offend. But sometimes I watch what happen on a white farm. It make me grieve, truly, it make me grieve, the ignorance about the land.
Bingham: For example, Mr Smart.
Smart: They plough, they plough the land. This soil here is like dust. When the wind blows, it disappears. In the air. You must treat it gentle, like a young girl. Then there is what they plant.
Bingham: Yes?
Smart: The whole land is just one crop. Perhaps that is good in England, but you cannot do that here. The rain —sometimes it is good, sometimes too strong, sometimes nothing at all. You plant maize and tobacco, good. Those are the crops for a good year. But you must plant sorghum and cassava, in case the rains fail. You must plant chick pea, to keep the soil fertile. There is a thousand things you must get right. I watch these white farmer crying because their coffee is destroyed by hailstorm and I weep for another reason, that they own the land and they don't know how to farm it.

Chairman: Do you have any other disadvantages in mind, Mr Smart?
Smart: You know, sir, you know full well, when I say the white people own the land, I mean we Africans have to work for them.
Chairman: You are speaking of immigrants from Portuguese East?
Smart: We are only immigrants since the flags came. Now, if we want land, we have to settle on a white estate. And we have to work for the landowner, six, eight months, with no pay, just to stay where we settle.
Mr Clunies-Rowland: That is not what the law of settlement says, Mr Smart.
Smart: That is what happen, sir, and why this rebellion happen.
Bingham: Let me be absolutely clear. You are attributing this rebellion, the primary cause of this rebellion, to the system by which immigrants from Portuguese East are allowed to settle on white-owned land in return for their labour?
Smart: Yes, sir.
Bingham: And you claim this labour is unpaid?
Smart: Yes, sir.
Bingham: And that it is exacted for periods of up to, what did you say, periods of six to eight months?
Smart: Yes, sir.
Bingham: And this is the primary source of dissatisfaction?
Smart: People say whites have taken the land. And that Africans have to work for them. And that this is slavery again, sir.
Bingham: Thank you, Mr Smart.
Chairman: Do you have any settlers on your land in Bangwe, Mr Smart?
Smart: Not settlers, sir. I have two cousins of my wife's.

Chairman: Do they work for you in return for the right to settle?
Smart: They work for me. But that is family, not land, sir.
Chairman: You see, Mr Bingham, Africans make marvellous lawyers. I sometimes think the legal profession is the truest proof of our African descent. But I would like to return to a question I asked you earlier, Mr Smart, and which you neglected to answer, namely, what were you doing in Ingode on August 10th? Were you expecting a consignment of boys?
Smart: No, sir. The last contract was in May. After that, all the boys were going to the war in the north.
Chairman: So what were you doing there?
Smart: I was there for my employer, sir.
Chairman: So your employer's letter stated. But what everyone seems to have overlooked is that August 10th was the date of the Battle of Nicuadala, when von Lettow-Vorbeck routed the Portuguese forces and looted the town. Are you asking us to believe your employers ordered you into the middle of a battle?
Smart: No, sir.
Chairman: You don't deny that the bulk of Ebenezer Chibambo's men came from Portuguese East?
Smart: That is true, sir.
Chairman: You don't deny that many Africans that side were fighting with the Germans?
Smart: I had heard that, sir.
Chairman: You don't deny Chibambo was trying to escape to Portuguese East when he was captured?
Smart: I did not know he was captured, sir.
Chairman: Answer the question.
Smart: People say he escaped to Portuguese side with a wound in his leg, sir.
Chairman: And there were you, conveniently located in Portuguese East, with no ostensible reason for being

there, on the very day the rebellion broke, a day when Namagoa Sisal could not possibly have required your presence in Ingode.

Smart: No, sir.

Chairman: I put it to you this was no coincidence. I put it to you that your real purpose was to establish contact with our German enemies. I put it to you Chibambo's plan was to invite German support for his fiendish rebellion and that you were his go-between.

Smart: Ebenezer never so stupid! He always know well German East worse than anything, worse than the Portuguese. He know well it is Muslim chiefs are sending men to Capitão Pauli. That is two enemies! He have enough troubles already.

Chairman: Then tell us what you were doing at Ingode?

Smart: I was afraid for my moneybox, sir.

Chairman: What moneybox?

Smart: The Company had a contract with some boys in July and they give me the money for the ganyão, eighty escudos. I sign the book for that amount, sir, and I hide it in a box under my bed. Then the contract cancel when the boys go up north as tenga.tenga with the army. When I hear Capitão Pauli was coming with his askari, I was frightened for the money. First, I go to Namacura. That is where I first see Mr Truscot, sir.

Bingham: Mr Truscot?

MacDonald: He was a missionary, Mr Bingham. Afterwards, he joined the Kings African Rifles.

Mr Clunies-Rowland: You saw Captain Truscot that day, the day he was killed?

Smart: I see him two times, sir. First was at Namacura, on the 9th. I ask his advice about the moneybox, and he tell me not to think of it. The Germans close by Ingode. That frighten me even more, because eighty escudos is too much money, too much money, sir. So I set out for

Ingode. My wife gone to Quelimane, but the money still there. It safe. I sleep that night at my house. Next day, I try to return. I have the moneybox under my coat. Then, just as I am crossing the stream, all of a sudden I hear guns, *pop pop, pop pop, pop pop*, all around me. I hide in the papyrus. I see the Portuguese and the English crossing, just further down where the stream join the river. Mr Truscot was with them. But just when he is almost across, he fall down. Then the Germans come in one big rush, *pop pop, pop pop*, and everyone is running, running away. And the Germans sweep past. I hide right there in the bush. I hide there all night. The hyenas come. Next morning, I creep out. Everything quiet, everything silent, not even birds singing. There were bodies lying around. I look for Mr Truscot, but I don't find him. I think they must have carried him away. So I steal through the bush, keeping away from the roads. I sleep a second night in the bush. On 12 August, in the morning, I give the money to my employer, Mr Corvo Branco. He is the one who tells me about the rebellion this side. Until then, it is the first time I have heard anything about Ebenezer Chibambo's rebellion. Also, I find out the Germans have gone back. Capitão Pauli burn Nicuadala and then turn back north. Then I decide to go to Quelimane and find my wife and take her back to Ingode. After that, I return to the Malosa border and that is when I get arrested.

After that, they didn't seem to want to ask any more questions. Mr Bingham asked if there was anything I wished to say. That's how he spoke, as though he was reading from a book, with spaces between the words. But I knew it was no use telling them how the soldiers burned my house at Bangwe, and burned my tobacco, and stole my iron bed and my Raleigh bicycle, and how Mr Barrow moved the survey markers when I was in jail. It was no use. Mr Bingham's proper procedure was not going to help me.

It was afterwards, not when I was in jail, but when I was back at Bangwe and was re-thatching my house, that I began thinking about the flags.

My mistake was to think they weren't real. That they were just a joke you could turn to your advantage, if you were smart enough. I thought, like Mavuso, you could play both sides and do good business at the same time.

But the flags had changed everything. They changed us. They drove Ebenezer crazy, with some vision of a place where he could rule righteously. There was no law that could help you if your flag changed. The whole war was about how fighting could change your flag.

It was after I had thought about all this that I started this tribal thing. There were no tribes before the flags came. But when the British looked at us they saw tribes, and if you belonged to a tribe they gave you space—not a flag of your own exactly, but at least a piece of land with lines round it. You have some influence over who's going to be chief. You collect taxes and have a treasury. You have native courts.

So I started this Achikunda Tribal Association (ATA) for the people who had come from Portuguese East. It's nonsense, of course. When we first came over, we didn't even speak the same language. But it's nonsense the British understand. My house is safe now. My tobacco has a market. I go to conferences with the governor. You are puzzled? You don't know who I am? Alec Mafambisse Chimilengo. That's right, I thought you'd recognize the name.

Man-eaters

In the Name of Allah, the Merciful, the Compassionate:
I, Faruch, came to this country of Africa
and found it indeed a strange place,
Many mountains, rocks and dense forests
abounding in gorillas and buffaloes,
With lions, giraffes, monkeys of every description,
and elephants impossible to converse with,
And rivers full of crocodiles and the water horse
and vast deserts where only the camel survives.
I found also strange trees
like the baobab growing upside down,
And strange flowers smelling like a woman's pudenda,
and strange peoples like the Bwana Sahib.
Now there is a railway winding and climbing,
bringing new things inland from the coast...

When I first saw him, Henderson Sahib seemed the strangest of all these strange sights. It was at Chinde, when we Indians jumped from the lighters and waded ashore. He was on the beach, giving orders about unloading the sleepers and the track and I'd had never seen anything like him. It wasn't just his physical presence—tall with big bones, and a brick red face and red knees, so that you wondered whether all the bits in between were red as well. You know what the Portuguese call the English? Bifes. Sometimes the word doesn't fit—they can be so pale the sun seems to shine right through them. But he was a beefsteak.

What was strange was his absolute authority. He didn't shout or rage or wield a whip or anything. He just spoke, and we watched everyone jumping. We jumped ourselves, splashing ashore and lining up our bed rolls on the sand. This wasn't just a matter of arriving in a savage place after crossing the black water. The truth is he expected it. When he spoke, he just took it for granted you would do as he said. And it lasted—oh, I don't know, three years, ten years? When I wrote that poem in strict metre, and we all combined to have it inscribed on a silver plate, I really had faith he was a hero. Like Sohrab, or Rustum, a man who could conquer the devil just like he outfaced the African sun.

Now, of course, with the Mahatma's teachings and all the scandal, he's just a man like you and me. But in those days, my belief was bigger. Or simpler, which is the same thing. Until now, after all these years in Africa, my faith was that the lions were real.

We'd come to Africa to build the railway, winding and climbing from the coast, like my poem says. Have you ever studied what a simple matter a railway is? When I think how we used to worship the white man. Yet he colonised us with such simple ideas. A necklace from a Bombay silversmith, or even sweets from Madras, take far more culture and skill. All a railway consists of is rails laid flat on the ground, with sleepers to bolt them in place, and an engine driven by boiling water. Why didn't we think of it first? Sometimes you have to level the ground, because railways are very feeble and can't run too much uphill. So you need labour to dig the cuttings. So you import Indians like us.

But you see the craziness? They have a simple idea, too simple for others to think of. It takes hard work to make it work. So they make others work to make it work. And in this story, they are the ones on top. It troubles me sometimes, waking at night. Why, when I know what a simple thing a railway is, did I so much worship Bwana Henderson?

Then I remember the lions. Did you ever hear a lion roar at night? Close by, when you're sleeping in a tent or a grass hut? Actually, if you hear him roaring you're safe because it means he's not stalking you. When they're stalking they're quiet as chameleons. But you don't think of that when the roar hits you. It hits you in the pit of the stomach, like the beat of the biggest drum you ever heard. It turns your inside to water. Afterwards, the little grunts and snuffles they go on making are like little earthquakes under your mat.

Worst of all is the terrible purring they make, when they're lying down and eating one of your friends. Three times I listened to that, close by in the dark. And then Henderson Sahib killed them.

In the beginning, I thought his passion for killing things was mad. Our first job was to get the rails and sleepers and all the crates of tools and equipment upriver from Chinde to the railhead—you understand in those days everything had to be imported from England. Leeds and Darlington it said on the boxes. Now I have a son in Leeds, studying to be an engineer. You see how the world changes.

To get them upriver, we had to build pontoons, unpacking the sections and riveting them together, following the numbers chalked on the separate parts. We got the hang of it quickly, and it was fascinating watching all the bits fitted together and turning into giant iron canoes. Then they were loaded with all we need to build a railway, and lashed either side of two paddle steamers, Venus and Minerva.

You see what a strange world we were in? The words we were hearing didn't fit with anything we saw.

The river was in flood and we only made ten or twelve miles a day. Sometimes the bwana travelled on deck, sometimes he walked along the river bank. Always, he carried two guns, and anything bigger than a cat he shot at. If we rounded a bend and a crocodile was sleeping on a sandbank, he shot at it. If a hippo stuck its pink nose out of the water and yawned like a piano, he let fire at it. If a herd of antelope came down to drink, he would stop the steamer downwind, and wade ashore to bag one. Afterwards, he would say, that's something 'for the pot' or that's one less 'loathsome creature'.

In his book, he says, one morning we saw an ostrich running along the bank and his friend Dr Meikle dropped it 'with a lucky shot'. It was 'a particularly fine specimen' and he had to order the captain to reverse the steamer to take it on board. I don't remember the ostrich, but that's exactly how the sahib was. Even in his writings, he took it for granted everyone would see thing as he did. Somewhere in the accident of all this, I found myself his gun-bearer. Allah knows, I never volunteered and I don't remember being chosen.

I don't know if you understand how railways are built? Clearing the bush and laying the rail is easy. All it takes is an eye for the country, and in that Bwana Henderson was expert. He could always see where to cut corners and save money for his bosses. The obstacles—cuttings or bridges—you arrange provisionally, and then come back to make secure. The result is the work camps are spaced out over fifty or more miles. Some of us were laying track, some clearing fresh bush, some widening cuttings miles back. This explains why the compounds were so strung out, and so unprotected. Most of them were only occupied for a few nights.

I was with sahib Henderson and the Pathans, bridging the Lualuba river. The Pathans were stone-masons. Or so they said. Some of them were stone-masons, but some were just Pathans. They were building the abutments, and the sahib had a lot of trouble with them because they were paid double for their skills and some of them hadn't any skills. Also, they needed women. For the workers who were moving up the line, this wasn't a serious problem because any trouble they caused was temporary. But the Pathans were there for weeks on end, and the men of the villages along the riverbank didn't like it.

That's what I believed because, you see, I was sure the lions were real. I knew there were quarrels and bad feeling, but the quarrels weren't with Henderson Sahib. There were rumours about a shrine the railway had knocked down with a cutting driven through a sacred grove. There was supposed to be a python god called Mbona living there, with his human wife that one of the Pathans had raped. I didn't believe it, and I didn't like it, because the story only started after one of the lions bit his foot and dragged him screaming through the thorns of our stockade wall, and feasted on him outside in the darkness while we all sat sick at heart and trembling. When the rumour started, it seemed they were saying it was justice and he had only himself to blame.

I don't remember any shrine. But in those days I was expecting something like a mosque, not just a granary no one had thatched for years. Perhaps Henderson Sahib did knock something down. It's not something he would have noticed.

Afterwards, oh this was all of ten years afterwards, there was the scandal about the safari and Bwana Littlejohn's death. Even then the lions didn't upset my faith. I got job as a type-setter with *The Planter*, and got married and opened an emporium—all the usual things.

Three sons and a daughter like a jewel. For a long time, life ran smooth. But now there's this stupid English novel, *Passion in the Jungle*, and it's amazing how stupidity can disturb you, and set you thinking.

Passion in the Jungle is by a lady called Cynthia Springer, and there is a picture of her looking very blonde and modern and smoking a cigarette. It is published by Jonathan Cape and cost 3/6d. The novel turns Henderson Sahib into Captain George Scott, an officer from the Indian Army but sent on duty to Nairobi. He doesn't like Nairobi because it's getting too much like Jo'berg—too many Jews and Indian shopkeepers—but when his time's up and he takes the train to Mombasa, he has second thoughts and wishes he had seen more of Africa. No lions, you see. No terror. Just sport, and rounds of bridge, and those passionless flirtations we Muslims find so hard to understand.

He's got some leave due, so he doesn't have to go home immediately. In Mombasa, he meets Joseph Spenser and his new wife Emma. Spenser is a millionaire, the son of a fertiliser manufacturer, but his wife belongs to an aristocratic family from Cornwall that has lost all its money. This is when it all becomes confusing for an Indian like me. I once worked in the Gymkana Club in Bangwe, fixing things—if the generator broke down or the lawn needed re-turfing, I was the man they relied on. So I used to study the English, and this novel reminded me of what I used to be hearing.

It's a bit like caste, but then it's not like caste. With caste, Emma would never have married Joseph. But although her family needs his money, Joseph's definitely wrong. He's trade. I understand that. But he was at Eton. There's a bit when Captain Captain George objects to

Joseph's wearing an Eton tie, and when he's told he was there, because you never know these days, Captain George exclaims, 'Good God, what are we coming to?'

Which Henderson Sahib, by the way, would never have uttered. He was too good at his job for an educated man.

Joseph and Emma want to go on safari, and Captain George agrees to manage it for them. I don't know why this isn't trade, but that's the English. Joseph drinks whisky, by the way, which is wrong, while Captain George drinks port like a gentleman. But the worst thing about Joseph—far worse than his Eton tie and his whisky and his general not knowing how to behave—is that he doesn't want to shoot animals. He just wants to photograph them. In his childhood, a very unhappy childhood, he used to read about Livingstone, and he wants to travel into undiscovered lands and take photographs.

Captain George finds this incomprehensible. He gets on better with Emma who is a good shot and is more like a boy than a woman. She's plucky and 'slender' (I think that means she's got no breasts) and she knows how to read a map. She thinks like a soldier. Often he praises her for being like a boy. I can tell you, Henderson Sahib was never that way inclined.

In my poem, I wished the sahib as his reward:

Ten virgins with teeth like pearls,
Eyes like the moon, and breasts like melons.

Instead, this English storyteller gives him a flat-chested woman with a shotgun and a pith helmet.

Does this seem funny to you? I thought it was funny. Anyway, they go on safari, through 'detestable places' in German East, getting lost, catching fever, facing a mutiny of the porters, attacked by a lion, doing all the usual things. Emma gets a good bag, while Joseph takes his photographs. And Captain George all the while keeps his stiff upper lip, thought secretly he's fallen in love with Emma, and she with him.

One day, after Joseph has had one of his whisky tantrums, he disappears. These tantrums were about his father and trade, and how his father drove his mother to her grave and how Emma was the only woman who ever understood him. But now he's gone, and for all his reconnoitres, Captain George can't find him.

What should the English pair do? Obviously, Joseph's dead, and from their point of view, good riddance.

What they do is separate for eight years. She goes back to Cornwall, he stays on in Nairobi. One day, when he's serving in a platoon pursuing the German general Von Lettow-Worbeck, Captain George stumbles on a skeleton in the bush. There's a watch and a locket with a twist of Emma's hair that identify it as Joseph's. Again, this couldn't happen. If Captain George could find these things, so could any passing hunter. But it seems like a happy ending. Captain George and Emma can marry. Except that Captain George dies of blackwater fever, so we're supposed to be in tears instead of laughing.

On Saturdays when my work at *The Planter* is finished and the emporium closes, I rest in a hammock hung between two mango trees in my courtyard. That's where, last week, I read this nonsense about Henderson Sahib. Him, not Captain George, because I know what really happened on that old safari.

And it offends me.

Henderson Sahib didn't have eloquence. When he shot the man-eaters, all he could say was that the first measured eight foot eight inches from tip of nose to tip of tail and stood three feet nine and a half inches high. The second was nine foot five and three feet eleven, its skin covered in scars from tearing through the thorn fences. He was describing Satan, and all he could write about was measurements.

But at least that was better that this gymkana club gossip. Because the author writes like she is a member of the club. If you're reading his book, you're supposed to belong too. Everyone agrees who's pukka and who's not. You don't have trade in your blood. You don't have tantrums. You bag animals, not photograph them. And you don't deserve a plucky wife who's like a boy with no breasts. As for the rest of world, well, it's made up of people who could never get to join. I mean wily Greeks and brutal Germans and greasy Pork-and-cheese, and rascally half-castes, and half-naked savages, and cheating Indian shopkeepers like me. None of us would ever get past the doorman, except to fix the generator or serve at table.

For ten years, I was alongside the sahib in his sport. Every head he bagged it was I, Faruch, who loaded and handed him the gun—.450 express with hard cartridge for elephant and rhino, .303 sporting rifle for antelope, and twelve bore shotgun for smaller game and the cooking pot. That's what I normally carried, though he also liked to use his Martini carbine. We didn't agree on this, because a Martini wasn't a big enough gun for a lion. I stalked with him, downwind, for hours at a time. I stood behind him, a little to the right, when we got close enough for the animal to charge—if he missed, the next gun had to be instantly ready on the instant. I was with him in the tree hide, taking turns keeping watch, when the man-eater stalked us the most frightening night of my life. It was I, Faruch, who first saw the pale patch of the devil's belly as he readied to spring. And I whispered and the sahib shot him.

I knew the sahib in danger, better than his own mother.

Now, in this stupid story, I'm just another chattering native. Not to be relied on, not admitted to the club. The Mahatma is right. All that has to change.

You remember the big drought in 1905? The Africans said it was the worst since Magumanya 'heap upon heap', but that was before our time. It was much worse on the Portuguese side than up here in the highlands, but even here some people starved. Old people for the most part, but women too because they had to stay with their land while the men could always go travelling to find work and food. They say it was that famine that first got people like Mr Barrow established as planters. After that, people knew they couldn't always depend on what they grew in their villages—it was better to have the double safe-guard of a job.

I'd been back home to get married and I was coming back upriver with my wife Muhsin to catch the train at Port Herald, when I first heard the stories. We had just come out of the marshes and round the bend to Mbame's village when Muhsin saw some green mangoes of the kind she likes to eat with salt. I remember she was delighted because although I had promised her there were mango trees in Africa, I don't think she had really believed me. So while we tied up so the cook could trade the coconuts he'd brought up from Chinde for the river fish we were to eat that night, I walked into the village and bought the mangoes.

Even there, on the lower river, you could see the effects of the drought. What hit me hard was that people there were blaming the railway. Trains had been running for just over a year then, if you remember, so I suppose it was natural people should make the connection. But then, after we settled in our new house in Bangwe, and I had planted those mango trees I told you about, I heard more.

The story was the python god was angry because we had destroyed his shrine and driven the railway through his sacred grove. The shrine had been there for centuries, and it was the god who controlled the rains. Every year in November, the chiefs and elders went to visit the grove and made libations of millet beer and prayed for rain. For three Novembers, that hadn't been possible because the python god was homeless. He was touring the fields at night, and blasting the crops to punish those who had let the railway be built.

'But why does the python blame his own people?' I asked. 'They didn't build the railway'.

I was talking with Mafambisse Smart, Paramount Chief Chimulengo he's now become. In those days we still traded in wild rubber and he used to bring me three dozen good-sized balls every time he came back from Portuguese side.

'But they don't stop it,' said Smart. 'They try. They try hard, but Bwana Henderson too much for them.'

'You're talking about the mutiny?' I said. 'But that was the Pathans, not the African workers.'

'I'm talking about the lions,' said Smart.

And so I heard about it properly for the first time. Smart had been to the Presbyterian mission school, but even so he told me like a man who was half impressed.

The man-eaters weren't really lions. They were the spirits of two chiefs, called Inhacatundu and Inhampindi. These chiefs had ruled before the coming of the Portuguese, and their descendants were still the chiefs and headman of the lower river. Inhampindi had fought with the Portuguese at Sena, and had been beheaded, like the priest who had been turned into the python. Inhacatunda hadn't died, but had climbed the mountain and ascended into heaven. It was these two spirits that had always prevented the Portuguese advancing into the highlands. So many Portuguese had been killed and eaten, they called the people of the lower river cannibals. But it was the lions were responsible.

When the British came, the python god said wait and see. The British were having a war with the Portuguese, so perhaps they might be our friends. Then the railway came, and it attacked the shrine. So the lion-chiefs fought back. Then, when Nyamayangu—that's what they called Henderson Sahib, it means 'the meat is mine'—when Nyamayangu's medicine proved too strong for the lions, the python god sent the drought instead.

'Do they say Henderson Sahib destroyed the spirits of the two chiefs?'

'No,' said Smart. 'He couldn't do that. But he destroyed the forms they took on and so they were helpless.'

I was thinking, as we talked, about Roshan. He was from the village next to my own, and on the sea voyage across the black water to Africa we became good friends. He used to joke about the money we were going to make and the wives we would marry. When I went home later, I went to visit his family and it was then that I met Muhsin. You see how things work together?

Roshan was sleeping in my tent when the lions came. I heard him shouting, 'Let go, let go.' And he was gone. Then there was the dreadful purring and grunting and crackling outside. Next morning, we found his head, his eyes staring at the mess of his flesh and bones. It was as though the lions had sucked off his skin and drank the blood before feasting on the parts they relished.

Next time this happened, with Hashid and Mohamed, I heard it all again. But I didn't go out next morning to look.

So when Henderson Sahib killed the lions, I saluted him.

As a brave and valiant man, like those Persian heroes
Rustum, Zal, Sohrab and Berzoor.
So brave is he that the greatest warriors stood
aghast at his action.
Tall in stature, young, most brave,
and of great strength is he.
Lions do not fear lions, yet one glance from Henderson Sahib
cowed the bravest of them.

It was strange, talking with Smart, to think the Africans believed the lions were the heroes. Even stranger, when I read this *Passion in the Jungle* to realise: for the gymkana club, this had nothing to do with the struggle between good and evil. It was just another local scandal, about a woman and two men, what they call the eternal triangle.

You think that's ingratitude speaking? Let me tell you what really happened on that safari with Mr and Mrs Spenser—it's an old story, we can keep those names, though you must forget all that caste business. Whether it was a good marriage or a bad marriage was no part of this tale. It's true Henderson Sahib regretted taking them along. The expedition was a survey, not a sporting trip, mapping part of the Dzalanyama plateau, and after three days it was obvious they were a hindrance. Mr S. had fever and had to be carried in a palaquin for hours at a time, while whenever the party met up with stray rhinos or a rogue elephant, the sahib had to pay as much attention to Mrs Spenser's safety as to the donkeys and porters. He wasn't after another bag. He was map-making.

After Mr Spenser shot himself and the safari returned to Bangwe without him, there was naturally a lot of gossip. Then, when Henderson Sahib wrote his book and told the simple truth—about how Mrs Spenser slept in his tent while he kept watch over Mr Spenser's fevers, and then how Mrs Spenser nursed him after Mr Spenser's death, it only made the gossip worse.

It was like his problem in describing the man-eaters. He gave simple facts, without explanations or atmosphere or understanding, and his readers filled in the gaps. So what began with the women in the gymkana club ended all these years later with *Passion in the Jungle.*

The plateau, too, had its sacred places. By this time, I'd been in Africa for eleven years and I took these matters more seriously. There were important rivers that had their springs up there, and you could find little clay pots with flour and millet beer in them, left for the 'little people' who had been the first inhabitants of this country. On the slopes of the plateau, there were shrines related to the one we drove the railway cutting through. Our mistake was to assume that because they were just bits of dry grass and mud, they didn't really matter very much. If they'd looked a bit more like a church or temple or mosque, the sahib would have respected them. But they just looked like the dilapidated granaries you could see in any abandoned village.

I see I'm confusing you. I said that for me the lions were real. I said I was going to describe that safari. When my wife Muhsin died in childbirth, I lost my head a little. Henderson Sahib was making the survey of the Dzalanyama plateau. He came to the emporium and invited me as gun bearer, and it was like starting in Africa all over again. To me, he hadn't changed, for all the white men I'd seen since. Cheats, fornicators, bullies. Henderson Sahib was still a beef, and heroic.

The difference was that I had started to think of the Africans as being a little bit like myself. This was long before the Mahatma's teachings, and it wasn't something I told my fellow Indians, because I wouldn't have been able to find the words for it. Most of the dealings between Africans and my countrymen were over the counter—or rather, through the window at the back that was for black customers. We saw hands with pennies in them, not faces and certainly not hearts.

So when we climbed up the steep, ferny gullies past the shrines and little sacrifices, and when we pitched camp for the first time and I heard lions roaring in the distance, I wasn't afraid, as I had once been. I thought, yes, this is the struggle for the land again. I wondered who would be triumphant this second time. And the answer is, Africa won. Not in direct confrontation, but by subtlety and stealth, just as it was that night in the lower river when the lions stalked us both, and only my sheer luck prevented them eating me. Africa won, more completely and effectively than anything that preacher Ebenezer Chibabambo could have achieved. Because Henderson Sahib was destroyed. Afterwards, he was never the hero again, except in my own sadness for the past.

Whodunit? I found that word the other day in an English newspaper. English is a wonderful language, always full of new inventions. The body in the library, the body in the tent. So who killed Mr Spenser?

In his book, Henderson Sahib says it was an accident. He says he discovered Mr S. always kept a loaded revolver under his pillow. If the sahib had known that, he would have acted sooner. Loaded revolvers could go off at any time. Mr Spenser was suffering from an attack of fever. He must have woken up, and felt for the gun, and it went off accidentally.

I saw Mr Spenser's body, with the skull shattered. The revolver had been pointed in his mouth and the trigger pulled. So, whodunit?

No, it wasn't Henderson Sahib, and it wasn't Mrs Spenser. As the novelist says, she was a like a schoolboy, with a flat chest and a chirpy approach to life. And she was brave, or as the book says, 'plucky'. When the rogue elephant attacked us, she was the first with her .450 that I, by the way, handed to her, loaded with hard cartridges. She was after a bag of her own, and Henderson liked her the better for it. Mr Spenser, by contrast, was a photographer, collecting pictures.

But there was never—what does Cynthia Springer say?—never any 'impropriety' between Henderson Sahib and Mrs Spenser. When you're on safari, living in tents, there are no secrets, least of all from your servants. We overheard every conversation and we could read every sign. Henderson Sahib was impatient with all the delays Mr Spenser caused, and he liked Mrs Spenser for being a good shot. But that was all.

So let me tell you now what happened. There is a disease here the Africans call chiwewe. The English call it rabies. The English say a rabid animal must bite you before you can get the disease. The Africans say if you look into the eyes of an animal you have just killed, you will be afflicted. Mr Spenser was forever staring into animals' eyes while he photographed them. I don't know how he caught the disease, but it wasn't any ordinary fever he was suffering from. And up there on the plateau, three weeks distant from Bangwe, he knew there was no cure. So he took his gun and shot himself.

That night, as Henderson Sahib says in his book, 'lions were roaring in all directions around our camp.'

The Mouse in the Anthill

A mouse in the anthill
Spoke some words.
Bwanas and donas,
Dig us out carefully,
You will cut our heads.

A mouse, look, that one,
Spoke some words.
Bwanas and donas,
Dig us out carefully,
Dig us out carefully,
You will cut our heads.

Break the anthill, very well,
    Break the anthill and eat us up
Ee break the anthill, travelling,
    Break the anthill and eat us up
You, mother, break the anthill,
    Break the anthill and eat us up
You, father, break the anthill,
    Break the anthill and eat us up

A mouse in the anthill
A mouse in the anthill
Spoke some words.
Bwanas and donas,
Dig us out carefully,
Dig us out carefully,
You will cut our heads.

Come out, one finger!
Come out, one finger!

Break the anthill, all right,
    Break the anthill and eat us up
Ee break the anthill, travelling,
    Break the anthill and eat us up
You, mother, break the anthill,
    Break the anthill and eat us up
You, father, break the anthill,
    Break the anthill and eat us up

The millet beer of Njawa
Is the best beer—ee,
The millet beer of Njawa
Is the best beer—ee
It's the beer that strengthens the drummer
It's the beer that strengthens the drummer
Beat the Gunde drum, my brother,
Beat the Wapanse drum, my brother,
I want the women of Njawa
To hear me—ee
I want the women of Njawa
To neglect their husbands—ee

A bad-mannered cockerel
Said to the guinea-fowl
Said to the guinea-fowl
Sorry my friend,
You are cold out there in the bush.

A cockerel with no manners
An educated cockerel
Said to the guinea-fowl
Said to the guinea-fowl
Said to the guinea-fowl,
Sorry, my brother,
You suffer out there in the bush.

The guinea-fowl replied
In want room.
The guinea-fowl replied
In want room.
For all your insults,
It's worse to be killed at home.

The guinea-fowl answered
In want room.
The guinea-fowl replied
In want room, for all your insults,
It's worse to be killed at home.
Mother, who has won ee,
    Who has won?
But the guinea-fowl
But the guinea-fowl today
Who has won?
But the guinea-fowl.
But the guinea-fowl
Who has won?
But the guinea fowl,
Who has won, brothers?
But the guinea fowl,
    Who has won, brothers
    But the guinea-fowl?

Heat the Gunde drum on the fire,
Heat the Ntewe drum on the fire,
I want the women of Mpinde
To hear me—ee
I want the women of Mpinde
To neglect their husbands—ee

A church elder
Has beaten a child
Has beaten a child
At a funeral
For the sake of ngaiwa
With utaka as relish

A church elder
Has beaten a girl,
Has beaten a girl, ee,
At a funeral
For the sake of porridge
With fish as relish
A church elder ee
A church elder
For the sake of porridge

Chikusiri drums are the sweetest drums
Ee, how can the feet be still?
Chikusiri drums are the sweetest drums
Ee, how can the feet be still?
The women of Njawa
Cannot resist the Wapanse drum,
The women of Mpinde
Cannot prevent the great Gunde drum
They will dance
Until their husbands are angry

They will dance
    Ee they will dance
They will dance
    Ee they will dance
They will dance
Until their husbands are angry,
They will dance
Until their husbands beat them,
Chikusiri drums are the sweetest drums
Ee, how can the feet be still?

The women of Bangwe
Have written me a letter,
Have written me a letter,
Dearest Mr Ngoleka
We should meet.

The women of Bangwe
The women of Bangwe
The women of Bangwe
Have written me a letter,
Dearest Mr Ngoleka
We should meet.

I answered her
Buladi fula!
I spoke to her
    Buladi fula!
I don't want your games
I am married.

The letter said
Dearest Mr Ngoleka
We should meet.
Buladi fula!

I answered her
Buladi fula!
Buladi fula!
I don't want your nonsense
I am married.

My wife, you, you, a-ya-a
  My wife, you,
My wife, you, you, a-ya-a
  My wife, you,
A man doesn't cheat himself, a-ya-a
  My wife, you,
I want to get a woman like me, a-ya-a
  My wife, you,
I am going to a church, a-ya-a
  My wife, you,
My church is a beer hall, a-ya-a
  My wife, you,
In Njawa they grow millet for beer, a-ya-a
  My wife, you,
Sister e—e, sister e—e
Let us rest.

Ofula

Tape no. 47: 16.30, 4 Oct, 1967
Interview with Mr Peter Rowland, aged 71,
Midima Village, nr. Bangwe, Zambwali.
His daughter Mrs Maria dos Santos assisting.

Hunter: Mr Rowland, it's a pleasure to meet you. My name's Lydia Hunter and I should explain I'm writing my doctorate for the University of Wisconsin on 'The Resistance to British Colonial Rule by Africans of Mixed-Race Descent'. I hope you don't mind my tape-recording this interview—just to keep the record accurate.
Rowland: Uh?
Dos Santos: That's all right, Mrs Hunter. You go right ahead.
Rowland: I bought this land. Forty-eight acres. I bought it in... in...
Dos Santos: 1932, Papa.
Hunter: Mr Rowland, may I—
Rowland: 1932. I went to see Mr Taylor at Lichinga. He was manager with the British Imperial Africa Company and I had heard that they were selling this land. Forty-eight acres. I had money, you see, from Namagoa Sizal. When the colonel, Mr Twining, told me I have to leave because they are closing the Cocorico plantation—afterwards they opened it again and I went back to work for the Company—but they gave me some money. £30. It was a lot in those days, and I bought this land from Mr Taylor.
Hunter: Mr Rowland, if I could—
Rowland: It's not my full name, you know. You can see it on the title deeds, Mr Peter Clunies-Rowland.

Hunter: Your full name?
Dos Santos: Our family name is really Clunies-Rowland. It was my grandfather's name. He worked in the administration here. But it's a bit of a mouthful so we just call ourselves Rowland.
Hunter: Mr Clunies-Rowland—
Rowland: Oh, Mr Rowland's fine. It's what I'm used to.
Hunter: Mr Rowland, when did you first become active politically?
Rowland: Uh?
Dos Santos: When did you start in politics, papa?
Rowland: We never had politics here. I never meddled in politics.
Dos Santos: I think the lady means when you stood in the election, Papa.
Hunter: Well, not—well, yes, okay, let's begin there. You were the leader of the Christian Democratic Party in 1958.
Rowland: All that was afterwards. I can't talk about that. I've already had too much trouble over that.
Hunter: But you fought the election. I've read your speeches.
Rowland: It was a mistake. Everyone said Life-President Kacheche was a communist. He was going to nationalise our houses and our land. Public ownership, they said. Whites, Indians and Coloureds. It was all a lie. After he became Life-President, everything was just the same. Independence, no difference. Communist, capitalist, I don't know. Perhaps the British were communists all along. Perhaps the Portuguese were communists. Perhaps that is why they came and took the Africans' land and made people work for them. Only I had to run away to Portuguese side. I had to run away three times. First, I had to run away from the British, after I had bought my land. Then I had to run away in 1961 after the election. Then I had to run away again in 1965, when the ministers made

all that trouble with the Life-President. Always the same running away, crossing the Ruo river at Volalo in the middle of the night with just a suitcase. Three times, leaving my land and my house.

Hunter: But you always came back, here to Zambwali.

Rowland: Three times I came back. The first time, I came by river in the steamer to Port Victoria, then by train to Bangwe. The second time, I came by train all the way. The third time, Senhor Coelho brought me in his car from Quelimane. It was Senhor Coelho told the Life-President I was too sick to cause any trouble. So Dr Kacheche let me come back here where you find me.

Hunter: Mr Rowland, in the National Archives—

Rowland: Uh?

Hunter: They have a building here in Bangwe where they keep old papers, old files and reports. Historians like yours truly have to work with these papers to find out about the past.

Dos Santos: It's that yellow building, Papa, in the old boma, just past the Likuludi turnoff.

Rowland: You mean Frederick's old place?

Dos Santos: They pull it down and put up this yellow building.

Rowland: I remember. What about it?

Hunter: It's where they keep old documents. I read your diary.

Rowland: Uh?

Dos Santos: What are you talking about?

Hunter: They have your father's diary from 1932.

Dos Santos: Diary? What is this? Did you ever write a diary, Papa?

Rowland: So those people still have it? And they allow someone like you to read it?

Hunter: It's a historical document. Anyone can read it if they get permission.

Rowland: You see what these people are like? Politics! A diary is supposed to be something private. After Mr Watkins searched my house and took it away, I looked it up in the dictionary. It said 'personal daily record' and 'private account'. Not something anyone can pick up and look inside.

Hunter: But when a diary is part of history—

Rowland: It's my diary. Like reading private letters.

Hunter: I assure you, Mr Rowland, I have done nothing irregular.

Dos Santos: Who is Mr Watkins, Papa?

Rowland: Oh, he's dead. Dead a long time back. He had that farm at the Thondwe junction. Before that, he was some kind of policeman.

Dos Santos: Why did he search the house? I don't remember this.

Rowland: It was 1932. You were just a baby. It was when I bought this land. There were some people living here, same as today but not so many. I mean Africans. They belonged to Henry Chimbambo's church. This was just after Reverend Sisulu came back from America to re-open it. I went to see him at the old boma—he had started the Native Association there—and explained to him what I was doing and how I didn't want any trouble.

Hunter: These people were thangata settlers.

Rowland: Thangata, yes. They were from Portuguese side. They had to work for the old company in order to settle on the land. I told Rev. Sisulu all that was finished. We made an agreement. The people could stay without thangata. If they worked for me, that would be a separate arrangement. I thought, good. There's plenty of land, for me and for them. We can live in peace. But it all ended with me running away, crossing the river at night with my suitcase.

Hunter: Mr Watkins wrote a report—

Rowland: He came to my house with three askari. He asked me, why did I buy my land here in Bangwe, where that rascal Chibambo lived? Why did I go to visit Rev. Sisulu? Why did I have such friends? Why was I joining the Native Association? Did I think I was a native, when my father was a hero? All these questions.
Hunter: He says in his report he found copies of *The Negro World.*
Rowland: Uh?
Hunter: Mr Watkins' report says he found copies of Marcus Garvey's newspaper, *The Negro World.*
Rowland: Probably he did. I read lots of newspapers in those days. *Time Magazine, The Planter, The African World.*
Hunter: Were you a subscriber?
Rowland: Uh?
Dos Santos: The lady means did you used to buy *The Negro World* regularly?
Rowland: It was Rev. Sisulu bought it, and he used to borrow me. But only at first. Mr Garvey wrote some things I liked. I knew he was a coloured, like me, though you American people call these things differently. He explained how coloureds have been cheated of our past. How it all started in Egypt, with the Pharaohs and the Pyramids, civilisation and progress, while white people were still living in the bush. He said the Sphinx had a broad nose like an African, like me, and that Napoleon damaged it because he didn't want people to know Africans could be civilised. Afterwards, I understood it was all just another kind of colonialism. All this Back to Africa business. He thought coloureds in America were civilised and would come to teach us how to behave. When I saw this, I stopped reading his newspaper.
Hunter: In your diary, you say: 'What is Egypt to us? If the Pharoahs were white and the Israelites were their slaves, then the Exodus story is about liberation. That's why Mr

Robeson can sing, "Let my people go". But if the Pharoahs were black, I would like to ask Mr Garvey this question. Were the Israelites the slaves of Africans? Are we supposed to be proud to have slave-owners as our ancestors?'

Rowland: You copied this out?

Hunter: And then it goes on, 'What if the Pharaohs were of mixed descent, just as they look in the tomb paintings? If that's how they were, no wonder they confuse people. I know the feeling.'

Rowland: I remember. Sometimes in those days we used to talk like this.

Hunter: Who used to talk like this?

Rowland: Oh, the Reverend Sisulu. And Aleki Smart, the old man Mr Barrow tried to steal his dambo land from. I forget who else. It was all a long time ago. In any case I had to run away.

Hunter: Did the authorities molest you?

Rowland: Uh?

Dos Santos: Did Mr Watkins start to make a case, Papa?

Rowland: I didn't wait around to see. You could get into bad trouble because of reading things. After that, I stopped keeping books. Even now, I just have the wireless.

Policia Internacionale de Defesa do Estado
Ficheiro No. 21987/50:
Sujeito: Pedro Afonso Clunies-Rowland:
Nacionalidade: Britannico:
Raça: mestiço:
Idade 52.

Documents no: 226, 257, 310, 358. 359 and 421 Numerador da Correspondencia Secreta attached.

1. Birth Certificate. Issued British Consulate, Beira, 10 June, 1911. Peter Clunies-Rowland, born 3 October, 1896, son of Geoffrey Clunies-Rowland and Asawilunda Muhinayula, nationality British. Place of Birth, Village Headman Kathupa's, Niassaland. Given under oath by Caroline Clunies-Rowland (née Thompson), 27 March 1911.

2. School record, unobtainable. The Misericordia have a file saying he attended the former Escola Serpa Pinto 1903-12 (destroyed by fire, 1923). In his application to the Namagoa Sizal Company, he claims to have completed the Quarta Classe Diploma.

3. Bilhete de Identidade (reproduced)

4. Letter from Col. Twining, Gen. Man. Namagoa Sizal Company, 23 Nov, 1931

Dear General Gago da Camara,

I am writing in support of Mr Peter Clunies-Rowland's application for an administrative post in the new government circumscription of Mangasanja.

I see from our records that Mr Clunies-Rowland joined Namagoa Sizal as a clerk in the Native Labour office in 1912. Due to the absence of many of our staff on war duty, he was promoted to compound officer in charge of the Nyasaland boys (he speaks fluent Nyanja). From 1921, he acted as field overseer, organising the tasks of work gangs engaged in planting and ditching (for which we employ Ngoni labour). His handling of the boys was entirely satisfactory, and it is with regret that due to the world recession we are forced, with the closing of our Cocorico plantation, to dispense with his services.

I am, sir, yours etc.

(Note: Pedro Clunies-Rowland was not appointed to the service)

5. Gov. Prov. Zambesia to Head Native affairs, No 487/38, with enclosures.

Your Excellency,

I forward a letter from Sr. Paiva de Fonseca, Chef do Posto for Dona Ana, in which he complains that many of the natives contracted by the Witswatersrand Native Labour Association (WNLA) are in fact of Portuguese origin.

These natives are from Zambesia, from the circumscriptions of Mangasanja and Migode. But they have in their possession documents issued by two mestiços, both fluent in Portuguese, the one based in Salima, the other in Bangwe, who are engaged in the clandestine recruitment of natives who have crossed the border illegally. From British territory, they travel to South Africa via the new railway bridge over the Zambesi at Dona Ana.

To the Good of the Nation
I am, sir, yours etc.

(Note: sub-delegação Native Affairs: enquiry in South Africa has established that Pedro Clunies-Rowland, then living in Bangwe, was employed by WENELA as a licensed recruiter.)

6. The following is certified to be an accurate copy of page 14 of the Relatório do Posto Administrativo de Inhacatundu, ano de 1949 (signed Henrique Barros Gomes, Notário).

Cultivators:

Pedro Clunies-Rowland, a mestiço but one of the better class and worthy of assistance, owns by legal title ten hectares at Doto on the river bank. He grows alternately rice and beans for sale to the Companhia Commercial, and is supplied with 5 workers each November (when labour is scarce) by this posto on three month contracts paid 60 Esc monthly plus posho. For harvesting and for the bean crop, he hires voluntary labour, mainly women. He is said to be of English origin, and worked for many years for Namagoa Sizal.

Dos Santos: What did you do when you got back Portuguese side, Papa?
Rowland: I was recruiting boys for woodcutting. I didn't have a license but I knew the work. Colonel Twining complained to the Governor, but when he found out it was me he thought better and he gave me my job back with the company. That way he kill two rabbits with one bullet.
Hunter: How long did you stay with Namagoa Sizal this time?
Rowland: Until the day I retire. I made sixty in 1956. October 3rd.
Hunter: October 3rd? Then yesterday was your birthday. Your seventy-first. Congratulations. Did you have a party?
Rowland: That was last year, when I turn seventy. But we had a little drink. My oldest son Geoffrey was here. He's got five children, two boys and three girls. They live in Salisbury but last year they couldn't come so this time they made the trip. Afonso, he's my second, was here with his wife, Betty. They have two boys at school in Johanneburg. Altogether, I've got seven boys and nine girls. Maria here is oldest daughter, after Afonso. Her husband works in Lourenço Marques. And fifty-seven grandchildren. Some

here, some in England, some in Salisbury and Northern Rhodesia, some Portuguese side.

Hunter: That's a huge family.

Rowland: They scatter. I used to think they would settle here. Sixteen children, forty-eight acres. That's three acres each. You can build a nice house on three acres. But they scatter. It's the modern world.

Hunter: And their mother?

Rowland: Uh?

Dos Santos: The lady wants to know about Mama, Papa.

Rowland: I married three times. The first wife, this one's mother, you'll find her living on the land, across the other side of the stream. I settled her there with her children when I bought the land in 1932. Then I married again, Portuguese side, and had seven more, three boys, four girls. I tried to settle her here, this side of the stream, two years before I retired. But she refused. She didn't like the situation, wife this side, wife that side, so she went back home to her plot in Doto. I married again when I retired here, and had two more children. But it didn't take. She left for Pirira five years back.

Hunter: One way and another, Mr Rowland, I have to say, you've been a bit of a lad.

Rowland: Uh?

Dos Santos: The lady's making a joke, Papa.

Rowland: It was the old way. When I saw Mr Taylor at Lichinga about the land, he said I was making a good move. The land was worthless because of the recession. But the recession wouldn't last for always. If I looked after it, it was sure to be a good investment. Being in an urban area, and so on. But I didn't look on it that way. I just wanted somewhere for my family. That was what you did. You earn some money, you buy land, and you have your family around. You build a village. Extended family, not just sons and daughters. I have my mother's sister living here even now. But those ways are gone. My family scatter, like the wind. But they keep my birthday without fail. Except two years back, when I had to run away because of the ministers, and Mr Coelho brought me back in his own car. I can't keep their birthdays—there's too many of them.

Hunter: Mr Rowland, you've had a long experience of British colonial rule and also of Portuguese colonial rule. Which did you find easier to tolerate?

Rowland: I remember my third daughter Caroline's wedding. Right there in the Sporting Club in Mopeia. A big affair. Her husband was working for accounts, so we were all in suits, hired from Beira. It cost me, meu Deus, it cost me my whole year's bonus. We had suits and dresses, and we had two bands. And food! Five goats, five suckling pigs, one big roast gazella I bought from the hunters, with samousas and sarapatel and—

Dos Santos: Papa, the lady doesn't know about such things.

Rowland: Anyway, Gonçalves were there, a coloured man from Ingode, some kind of cousin of my wife's. With a top hat, and pointed shoes, and tails—you know how coloured people can be. Well, maybe you don't, but that's how the man was Gonçalves, looking like Fred Astaire, and everything hired down the railway from Beira and due back with the return train.

Hunter: Mr Rowland, about tolerating—

Rowland: Afterwards (laughing), he gave me the jacket to send back, all covered in grease and stinking. I say to the man, what happened? He tell me he never did see such a banquet. Five goats, five suckling pigs, and suckling pig his very favourite. He take one of the pig's head and hide it under his jacket. He hide it there all through the wedding, the speeches and dancing and everything, until he could take it outside and feast himself.

Hunter: Mr Rowland, were you ever in any trouble with PIDE?
Rowland: I told you already, big trouble. In 1961, when I had to run away after the election. They arrested me in Mocuba and took me to jail in Quelimane. They had this big file on me—birth certificate, letters, reports—a bit like you, really, asking me about my diary after all these years.
Hunter: Thank you, Mr Rowland, for your time.

Resumé 16 Oct: interesting Negro World circulating in Bangwe early 30s. Otherwise disappointing. Patriarchal, few real political instincts, & entirely obsessed with land and family. Yet another coloured collaborator, even with the Portuguese. It might be amusing to mention I was compared with PIDE.

Policia Internacionale de Defesa do Estado
Ficheiro No. 21987/60:
Sujeito: Pedro Afonso Clunies-Rowland:
Nacionalidade: Britannico:
Raça: mestiço:
Idade 62.

Documents no: 875, 877, 1033 and 1211Numerador da Correspondencia Secreta:

1. Your Excellency,

I have had a meeting with one Pedro Clunies-Rowland, a British-born mestiço who speaks excellent Portuguese being a former employee of the Namagoa Sizal Company. He is currently in Quelimane under pretext of a holiday, trying to organise support for the Christian Democratic Party in Niassaland. I should mention that he brought with him letters of recommendation from the Archbishop of Niassaland and consul Coelho de Sousa.

The party is an alliance of Goans, Hindus, and Mestiços who feel threatened by Milton's Kacheche's People's Party, and has already received funds from the African Association here.

I recommend to Your Excellency that further discussions are appropriate, with the possible end of giving clandestine support to the Christian Democratic Party as a means of combating communism.

Mr Clunies-Rowland reports that there is considerable friction within the People's Party, especially between Milton Kacheche and the younger firebrands.

To the Good of the Nation,
I am, sir, yours etc.

2. Your Excellency,

Following my discovery that a branch of Milton's Kacheche's People's Party was operating in Mangasanja, I am happy to report that all elements have been arrested.

It may be of interest that members were identified by a double handshake, involving the entwining of thumbs, and that they employed the password Ofula.

To the Good of the Nation,
I am, sir, yours etc.

[Note: Dictionário da Lingua Nyanja, ed. Padre Francisco Ferreira: Ofula, to carve, to cut, to strip (e.g., barkcloth), to dig gently (e.g., dig a mouse from an anthill), to castrate.]

3, *The Gymkhana Club,Bangwe*
10 June 1960

My Dear Afonso,

Mr Rowland, as we know him here, is no Passover lamb but he's not *per se* unworthy of your support.

He first came to our notice in 1932 when he purchased forty-six acres of land near Bangwe from the British East Africa Company. This was all completely above board (he'd been given a pay-off by Namagoa Sizal, who'd employed him since schooldays), but Bangwe's always been a bit of a hot potato for this administration so we had to sit up and take notice. (Bangwe was the headquarters of Chibambo's 1917 rebellion, but there's no evidence Rowland was in any way involved.)

In 1930 one of Chibambo's disciples had applied to re-open his mission. Given Portuguese policy on such missions, you'll be surprised that we felt it was better to acquiesce. But to be honest, there were always doubts in our mind about the justice of the events of 1917—and it would be absurd to comment further. Rowland's only link with this development was that he was detected importing some of Marcus Garvey's newspapers. I read his confiscated diary and felt that while his political interests were genuine, they were academic and had no subversive content.

In 1937, he returned to work at Namagoa Sizal, remaining there until his retirement in 1951 at the age of 55. During the 1953 riots, he was entirely loyal to this administration, heading a militia that helped to check the worst excesses in the outskirts of Bangwe. His Christian Democratic Party was founded within three weeks of Milton Kacheche's return in 1958. If industry and commerce are to survive contemporary disturbances, it will be in no small measure due to his contribution.

This is, of course, my personal opinion. The chief objection to supporting his party is that you will be backing a loser. They haven't a hope of winning a single seat. Only the event will prove whether you or I are right. I look forward to drinking vinho verde with you in Mocuba next month.

Warm regards.

4. *Policia Internacionale de Defesa do Estado*

I have read this file with alarm that such a manifestly dangerous individual should long have evaded our surveillance and should now be beyond our jurisdiction.

I am also concerned by Mr (sig. illeg.)'s letter to Eng. Paiva Afonso. It is, of course, a private letter but I am disturbed by the degree of intimacy that exists between a member of our administration and a British official who appears to believe that Communism will prevail.

To the Good of the Nation
I am, sir, yours etc.

End of file, 23 October 1960

Fly Whisk

Whining like mosquitoes in the concrete cavern of Independence Hall, the cadences of the national anthem died querulously away and the tape-recorder was switched off. There was a rash of suppressed coughing, a scraping of metal chairs as the delegates resumed their seats. Dr Krishnamurthy Patel, Professor Human Relations at the University of Zambwali, rose to address the conference.

'Your Excellency, Mr Vice Chancellor, Representatives of the Peoples' party, Members of Parliament, distinguished guests, ladies and gentlemen. We are privileged—' He half turned to Life-President-and-National-Redeemer Kacheche. 'It is an honour that the opening session of this conference on the history of Zambwali should be addressed by the creator and Life-President of our beautiful and historic nation. Indeed, it s fitting.'

Professor Patel mopped his forehead with a paper tissue, wishing the English language permitted greater emphasis.

'Without you, Your Excellency, there could be no Zambwali, no glorious climax to the history we, under your enlightened patronage, are privileged to study. For the study of history—'

But Life-President-and-National-Redeemer Kacheche wasn't listening. During his first benign survey of the audience of dignitaries and visiting academics, he had suddenly removed his dark glasses and glared at one of them. Impatiently, he gestured with his fly whisk to the Minister of Home Affairs sitting behind him on the platform.

'Name!'

'I don't know, sir.'

'Ask Bennett.'

'For the study of history,' continued Professor Patel, 'in a territory such as ours, is the study of progress and development, the study of human dignity and self-assertion. You, Sir, who graduated from a humble village deep in the heart of our traditional homelands, and who rose via the gold mines of the south, the universities of Scotland and Canada, and not least via Her Majesty's prisons—' He looked up from his notes, smiling, coaxing a ritual titter from the British delegates—'You who thus rose to the highest office in the land understand better than any of us, professional historians though we may be, the progress we have made under your wise leadership.'

Impassively, the Vice Chancellor, a grey-faced Irishman with a year of his contract to run, scribbled a question-mark on an envelope and handed it to the minister of home affairs, who sat back on his haunches, his face a caricature of puzzlement at the information thus presented to him. Worry narrowed his eyes as he crept back to the Life-President's side.

'See to it,' Life-President-and-National-Redeemer Kacheche ordered, without bothering to lower his voice. He glowered again at a young, pinkish man sitting near the back of the hall. As delegates turned to follow the Life-President's glare, he blushed through his freckles and studied his conference programme through black-rimmed spectacles. Limp carroty hair lay lank across his collar.

Professor Patel sweated on. 'You, Sir, understand better than any of us the need to cherish the traditions you have forged, the need for an equal and open dialogue between black and white to ensure that this progress continues unimpaired.'

His voice climbed to near falsetto as he reached his peroration.

'Sir Winston Churchill, John F. Kennedy and Dr Milton Chiume Kacheche have all declared that the past is the key to the present. No man can escape his background. No man can deny his manhood. Or his womenhood,' he added, departing from his notes on a sudden thought. 'Or hers. Her womanhood'.

He turned again to the Life-President who at last acknowledged the occasion, detaching himself with a smile and a gracious inclination of his grey head from the events taking place in the hall. An embarrassed policeman, like an elephant on tiptoe, eased his hips noisily between the rows of metal chairs and led the offending delegate to the exit.

'We, Sir, delegates to this conference on the history of Zambwali, are proud to receive the patronage of a historian more venerable than us all, a maker of history whose achievements will never pass from the record.'

Now grinning broadly, Life-President-and-National-Redeemer Kacheche replaced his dark glasses and rose to reply. Applause from the visiting delegates was overtaken by the ritual accelerating clapping of members of the Zambwali people's Party as the Life-President waved his fly whisk, the symbol of chieftaincy.

'U – HU – R U!' he bellowed.

'Uhuru', shouted the ZPP members, breaking into ululations which drowned the noise of the exit doors clanging behind the policeman and David Springer.

Springer had been out of his depth ever since arriving in the Republic of Zambwali three months earlier. He had come on a two-year contract with the Zambwali Broadcasting Corporation as assistant-head of schools' broadcasting. At the airport, confronted with two queues at immigration, one of whites, the other much longer of blacks and Asians, he had demonstrated his commitment to the principle of racial equality by joining the queue of returning nationals. An hour later, when the Africans in front of him had been interrogated about their political contacts abroad and the Asians had been looted of their purchases, Springer reached the desk.

'What you doing here? You is on contract, isn't it?'

'Yes, sir.'

'Other desk'

But by this stage, the official responsible for processing work permits had gone back to the hotel bar, and the man from ZBC sent to pick up Springer had assumed he must have missed the flight.

Springer bought a Ford van, the Greek dealer persuading him it was ideal for travelling and sleeping up-country. Four days after he bought it, a taxi crashed into his rear at a junction. Springer took full responsibility. Without waiting to hear any charges, he admitted to careless driving, believing that the spectacle of a white man accepting black justice without complaint would draw an equally generous response. The affair cost him eight-thousand Zambwalian dollars, in those days some £400. He also had to put up with abuse from the taxi driver, who was convinced he was being persecuted in some obscure way.

Worst of all, however, were his daily confrontations with his house boy. There was no escaping Precious Kuntambila. Springer had known that in his heart of hearts the first morning he opened the door of his fourth-floor government flat and found the tiny smiling African on his doorstep asking for 'a work'. That first morning, Springer explained he didn't intend to employ a domestic servant. He didn't believe in societies with two distinct economic levels and had no intention of giving the immorality of class distinctions the support of his collaboration.

The second morning (Springer assumed it was the same man, though he wasn't absolutely sure), he said that the spectacle of the black man serving the white man was offensive to him, that Zambwali was no longer a British colony, and that it was he who had come to serve. He could not agree to perpetuate, on however lowly a level, the exploitation of the past.

The third morning, with his dirty underwear beginning to pile up, he pleaded that his salary as assistant head of a tiny unit would not permit him to pay what his conscience required. To employ a domestic servant at a mere £1.50 a week, and to allow him to live in the squalid brick huts that were the servants' quarters, was repugnant to him.

Precious did not argue. He simply reiterated that he wanted 'a work'.

'No work. No money. No food,' he said periodically, ignoring even the pauses in Springer's explanations.

He took possession of the doorstep, living there permanently, intercepting Springer whenever he came out or went in, and brandishing a scrap of paper which declared he had been trained in South Africa and was 'as clean and as reliable as any of them are'. It was an effective campaign and Springer knew he was losing.

The fourth morning, he had a disaster. For all his goodwill towards the black man, Springer was nervous about burglars. Every night he locked all the doors, counting them and double-checking, before hiding the keys under his bed. But the passage door had a self-locking mechanism. Once the arm had been set, it could only be opened from the inside. Springer had made his coffee on the fourth morning and was opening the living room louvers when the wind slammed the passage door shut. He was trapped three storeys high, with all his keys locked away in the bedroom.

He looked down from the window. The car park was deserted. He sat down and drank his coffee. Then he fried himself an egg. He tried to pick the passage door lock with a paper clip and then tried to force it with the bread knife. Finally, he listened for a few minutes at the front door.

'Precious,' he called.

'Yes, master.'

It was an enormous relief to hear his voice. Half an hour later, Precious returned with the government housing officer, a tanned, huge-boned Rhodesian in a safari suit. He betrayed no surprise at finding Springer still in his pyjamas as he opened the door with a master key.

'You satisfied with this boy? He's not getting out of hand?'

Springer bristled.

'Yes. No. Yes, sure, okay, he's fine.'

'Come over for a beer some time.'

Heroically, Springer made a last effort to retain control. He told Precious he was taking him on part time at half pay. Precious would have certain duties—washing, ironing, and dusting—but as soon as he had finished work his time was his own. If he wanted to find other part time jobs, that was fine.

Precious agreed to everything. For a whole month, he worked hard to prove that looking after Springer was a full time job. He turned up for work at 5.00 am, banging noisily about the kitchen, and didn't go back to his quarters until after he had washed up Springer's dinner things. He found clothes to wash every day and ironed them with geometric precision. He prepared elaborate stodgy meals, explaining he had learned about white man's food in South Africa. He took responsibility for the shopping and Springer found himself saving money. Gradually, he induced Springer to surrender more and more of his habits of cleanliness. Precious rushed to make the bed while his master was shaving. Then he dashed to the bathroom and sighed and sucked his teeth because he found the basin already rinsed and the bath cleaned and the toilet flushed. Springer, eating his burnt toast and an egg boiled blue, felt intimidated. Precious had other advantages. His very name suggested indispensability. His size made Springer feel a bully to deny him anything. His forty years and his long experience in the racist south made Springer, who was just twenty-three, feel deferential. By the third week of this, Springer found himself knocking out his pipe on the tiled floor of the living room and leaving empty beer bottles under his bed. The African's beaming response was that of a schoolmaster whose most backward pupil has at long last got the point. Springer showed promise of becoming a real bwana. Precious was engaged full time at £8 a month, with a weekly bar of soap and a weekly food ration thrown in.

Waiting in the car park outside Independence Hall, Springer was once again at a loss. Never since he was appointed head boy at Birkenhead Institute (an achievement of which he was deeply ashamed) had people paid so much attention to him.

'They should give you forty-eight hours. How are you fixed tomorrow evening?'

'Good for you. It's high time somebody stood up to these people.'

'It would be so nice landing at Heathrow the day after tomorrow.'

Springer had, in fact, spoken to very few people since his arrival. Being passionately opposed to imperialism and the past, he refused to join the country club and steered well clear of his white neighbours. Since most Zambwalians had their own concerns, which they preferred to conduct in their own language, this left him with virtually no one to talk to.

A few ex-pats dropped in to invite him for drinks. They told him this was the dry season, an unusually dry dry season, though not so dry as their own first dry season when the Africans were dying like flies. He was taken for drinks at the High Commission where attempts were made to recruit him to the sailing club, the mountaineering club, the rugby club, the music society, and an ex-serviceman's association called the Memorable Order of Tin Hats which arranged cheap charter flights to Britain. (He did, in fact, visit this club and drank tepid beer while a juke box played 'Roll Out the Barrel' and 'It's a long way to Tipperary'. For the rest of his stay in Zambwali, he received a monthly newsletter beginning 'Dear Blokes'). Then a newsreader at ZBC took him to one of the new game parks, where (this being an usually dry dry season) they sat in a hide by the waterhole and were rewarded in the late afternoon by the sight of three labourers coming to cut down a tree. But after about a fortnight of this, the white tide ebbed and he was left to his own devices.

Until now.

Standing in the shade of a flamboyant tree where the policeman constable had told him, 'You stay, bwana,' Springer found himself the hero of the hour. He was joined immediately by Dr Van Leiden who occasionally took part in the daily five-minute devotions which preceded the schools' broadcasts. Dr Van Leiden had come to Zambwali as a catholic missionary and stayed on as an anthropologist. His paper on the madzahari cult, a secret dung-eating society of which he was a member, was due to be presented at the history conference as a case study of resistance to British rule. An observer, always observing, he stood by silently as Springer listened to the earnest exhortations of a serious, dark-blue suited young man who had followed him out of the conference hall.

'Rogers. High Commission, Third secretary. Have you signed the book? You ought to, just for the record. Well, I'm afraid there's not much we can do. Our hands are tied, you understand. Wheels within wheels. In confidence, I can tell you last time we complained the president refused to speak to us for six months. We'll see you're protected of course. Drop in before you leave and give us your version of the affair. Just for the record.'

He disappeared back into the conference hall.

'Do you know him?' asked Springer tentatively.

'He's been here a couple of years,' said Dr Van Leiden, a little reluctant to commit himself. 'Not important. Those people know very little of what's really going on here.'

'What did he mean about my leaving?'

'He assumes you're going to be deported.'

'Deported! Good God, will I?'

'Who knows?'

'But surely, I mean, what have I done?'

'Who knows?' repeated Dr Van Leiden. 'We all have to believe it's something sufficiently serious. Few people ever know what's really going on here.'

'But they can't throw me out for no reason.'

Springer was close to tears. He deeply wanted to learn, not simply how he had offended, but to discover the mainspring of this African society, to share the extraordinary knowledge Dr Van Leiden had accumulated. Humbly, he stared across the car park, where the black and maroon Mercedes-Benzes belonging to ministers and party officials were drawn up at an appropriate distance from the VW Beetles and Renault 4s from the university college. The Benzes, whose white-gloved drivers paced proudly beside them, shooing away children and polishing invisible specks of dust, had velvet cushions in their rear windows and little plastic dogs with bobbing heads. The university cars were covered with sticklers for Serengeti and Gorongosa game reserves.

Beyond, in the shade of purple-blazing jacarandas, sat members of the Women's Congress, a thousand or so dressed identically in bright cotton prints, each featuring a youthful looking Life-President Kacheche and the ZPP watchwords of Unity, Obedience and Production. The women were brought in by the lorry-load from surrounding villages for every state occasion. Now, having sung and danced and ululated the Life-President into the conference hall, they sat patiently in groups, talking, smoking, re-working the intricate squares of each other's hair styles, or suckling their babies at pendulous breasts, until it was time to dance and sing and ululate their Redeemer back into the presidential limousine and they could return to their husbands and maize gardens.

Feeling on the verge of a revelation, Springer gazed at the women and at the rows of flagpoles, many hundreds of them spaced at tem foot intervals, lining the road curving over the rise towards the capital.

'That's why you've got to go,' said a flat, nasal voice, and Springer turned to see the government housing officer, his safari-suited rescuer.

'The flag,' he explained. 'Black for exploitation, red for the martyrs, blue for the lake, and white for the flagpole that's keeping the whole show on the road. That's why they kick one of us out from time to time. It kids them we're not really indispensable.'

Again, Springer bristled inarticulately

'You never came over for that drink,' said the Rhodesian. 'Make it tonight. First house on the right after the country club.'

'And then come on to dinner with us.'

'Come and get drunk. I do enjoy deportations.'

'I think it's romantic. It makes you seem very important.'

'What have you decided to do about your car?'

Where had they all come from? Was the Life-President left without an audience? Like gods in a Greek epic, exercising power but subject to the irrational fates, the clustered around Zambwali's latest victim.

Dr Van Leiden stood by, observing in silence.

But Springer was not deported. After three quarters of an hour, he was rescued by Banda, his newsreader friend from ZBC. He was driven into the capital to a barber's shop where his carroty hair was clipped short by the Portuguese owner. Then he was taken to the Delhi Bazaar to be fitted out with a navy-blue blazer, grey flannels and a dark tie. They dropped in briefly at the Continental for the double whiskies the occasion seemed to demand. Finally, they arrived back at Independence Hall just as the Life-President-and-National-Redeemer was finishing his speech. Springer caught sight of himself in the men's room mirror.

'Christ,' he said aloud. 'I look just like Ian Smith.'

But Life-President Kacheche was satisfied. He gave Banda and Springer a curt nod of approval as he walked through columns of ululating women to his limousine.

'The curious notion that Zambwali was "discovered" by Dr David Livingstone,' ran Professor Patel's cyclo-styled discussion paper for the history conference is only the first of many colonial myths which must now be rejected. One might just as well argue that one day in 1859, a day very much like any other, the Zambwalian people "discovered" Europeans walking across their ancestral lands. There can be little doubt that they recorded the event in their own inimitable ways.'

The professor paused, biting his lip. Was this the right note? Should he not have worked in a reference to the Life-President? Perhaps after the date 1859 he could insert 'a mere thirty-nine years before the birth of etc.' But the Life-President's age was a dangerous topic. He read on.

'It is also necessary to refute the heresy, promulgated by Hegel and Karl Marx and Hugh Trevor Roper, that Africa has no history or, conversely, that her history begins with the first written records kept by Europeans. Now that indigenous peoples are at long last being questioned about their past, a glorious past which they have always documented in their own inimitable ways in archaeology and oral traditions, it is becoming increasingly clear that contact and dialogue with the outside world did not begin in 1859 but has been a central feature of Zambwalian history for many centuries. Dr Coleman's excavations at the Kapuchiri burial mounds have revealed sea shells of great antiquity which can only indicate extensive trade at period before Christ with communities a thousand miles away on the east coast and beyond across the Indian ocean.'

Professor Patel checked his footnotes:

Soc.Zam.J. (1967), 23-7: it will be apparent that I reject Dr Christie-Swanzie's suggestion that the Kapuchiri burial mounds are anthills and that the shells are of geological not historical significance.

'The first event of significance to modern historians of Zambwali, however, was the arrival here of a Bantu-speaking people shortly after the Norman Conquest. Travelling south-east in waves from the ancient empires of northern Angola, as the linguistic evidence clearly demonstrates, they quickly displaced the less technologically advanced Akafula (the so-called Bushmen) who were no match for their conquerors. The settlers brought with them culture and the traditional skills of their forefathers and quickly established a peaceful and high-structured society extending over an area much larger than the artificial colonial boundaries of present-day Zambwali. The country was ruled then by an emperor, who governed with the assistance of an aristocratic class of elders, together with priests and rainmakers, and of regional paramount chiefs each with their own deputies and other persons of high rank, right down the the humblest, hard-working peasant. These people were the ancestors of the present day Azimba tribe, the largest and most influential in modern Zambwali, whose most distinguished representative is our beloved Life-President-and-National-Redeemer, Dr Milton Chiume Kacheche.'

Thank God he had held back his handout until after the Life-President's opening address. His first draft had spoken of pre-colonial village democracies where land and property were held in common and all ate from the same pot under the benign authority of the elders. But the Life-President had shouted that 'We, too, had knights and squires and viscounts and marquises and earls and lords and lord lieutenants' and he had made all Zambwalians present take an oath that anyone who claimed Africa didn't have knights and marquises and lord lieutenants just because it wasn't written down anywhere, would be reported to him personally.

Professor Patel turned the page.

'The Azimba were followed in later centuries by the Nyakusas migrating from the north, the Ajawa from the east, the Mazitu from the west and the Nyungwes from the south. Throughout this whole period, contact and dialogue—' (Good. He'd got they key phrase in twice) 'with the outside world was maintained first with the Arabs, who brought cloth, rice and mangoes in return for ivory and free migrant labour and, from the seventeenth century onwards, with the Portuguese who appropriated the gold mines inside what were our original boundaries. The measured progress towards a humane African industrialism was accelerating after 1850 but was rudely interrupted by our European invaders. It should be noted in passing that the harmful effects of the so-called Arab slave trade have been much exaggerated by those who gained from the pretence that colonialism was beneficial. The denigration of those chiefs who understood the benefits of foreign trade must now be seen in fuller perspective as part of the policy of divide and rule.

'What has aptly been termed "the colonial interlude" began for Zambwali in 1890. Unlike other African territories, Zambwali suffered little by way of mass white immigration. We had our quota of missionaries, undermining our traditional customs. We had numerous settlers, depriving us of our ancestral lands. But there were no industrialists to develop our economy, and British rule did virtually nothing to improve educational standards or to stamp out ignorance, poverty and disease. What must be emphasised is that the imposition of colonial rule ushered in a long period of national resistance during which the initiative lay always with the African. British policy may be characterised as an extended rearguard action, stifling the developing instincts of Zambwalians to express themselves economically, socially and above all politically. It became increasingly clear, however, that the British had to be resisted in their own terms. The abortive rising of Easter 1917, though manifestly heroic, was far too backward and tribal in its methods to hope for success in the modern world. Not until 1957 when the then Mr Milton Kacheche promulgated the watchwords "Unity, Obedience and Production" was it apparent that a statesman had arisen among us destined to rid us of the oppressor. Our beloved Life-President-and-National-Redeemer, who has suffered much ingratitude from confusionists and tribal gangsters, accomplished this in just seven years. At midnight on April 1st 1964, Zambwali returned to its position of pride in the comity of nations.'

The professor of Human Relations finished reading the stencils with a sigh of relief. This time there were only five typing errors. It would have to do. He arranged for it to be run off on the Gestetner. They would be ready in plenty of time for the Vice Chancellor's cocktail party for conference delegates.

'Another deportation today,' said Professor Hicks, holding his glass of South African sherry dubiously against the light.

'Well, he was asking for it wasn't he?'

'What had the young fool been up to?'

'It seems,' said Hicks, 'there was some plan to blow up bridges. All tied up with the trouble across the border'.

'I heard it was something to do with a schools' broadcast. Something that was said about Livingstone not being entirely trustworthy.'

Springer opened his mouth to comment, then closed it quickly and took a sip of sherry. Nobody seemed to recognise him in his new rig.

'Well,' said the Vice Chancellor, draining his glass with a pained look and preparing to circulate, 'there's no need for us to express an opinion. For once, thank God, it's none of our concern'

‘Yes,’ said the Vice Chancellor to Lydia Hunter, lecturer in social psychology, who was tilting the bottle for him, ‘it really is barbaric. There’s absolutely no excuse for giving a man just forty-eight hours.’

‘He seems,’ said Dr Hunter, ‘to have been singularly inept.’

‘Oh, quite.’

‘If you’re after drugs in this country,’ said Dr Hunter, ‘the first thing you must do is square your house boy.’

Professor Patel, looking more than usually sheepish, was scurrying about the room distributing copies of his handout on Zambwali’s history, when Professor Lambkin arrived with an unexpected African guest.

Professor Lambkin was the star of the conference. This was only his third visit to Zambwali. He had dropped in once for three days in 1948 en route by flying boat to Southern Rhodesia, and he had spent a week in the capital as a guest of the new government during the independence celebrations. As a result, from his secure post in Aberdeen University, Professor Lambkin ran Zambwalian history. All research on Zambwali was wise to seek his stamp of approval. All appointments in related subjects were channelled through him. All documents surfacing about Zambwalian history were deposited by special arrangement in his university’s special archive. All journals covering the area as a whole consulted him about articles submitted for publication.

He had made his name with a book about the 1917 rising. Making use of materials supplied by friends in Zambwali but writing in Aberdeen, he had constructed a simple story of educated, progressive, nationalist-minded rebels provoked beyond endurance by colonial settler exploitation, but committing the unfortunate historical error of being years ahead of their time.

Professor Lambkin, in sharp contrast, was very much in tune with his times. The book had been published during the interim period of internal self-government which preceded full independence and it became wildly popular in Zambwali. It wasn't read there—it wasn't officially permitted to go on sale since the new administration found itself strangely reluctant to allow into the country a book celebrating an anti-government revolt. But it was referred to frequently in the speeches of Prime Minister Kacheche, as he then was, and extracts appeared in the party newspaper. For a few weeks, Mr Kacheche even took to walking with a limp, hinting at physical identification with Ebenezer Chibambo, charismatic leader of the 1917 rising who was shot in the leg before his ascension into heaven.

Curiously, the book's popularity had little to do Professor Lambkin's attack on British colonial policies, much more with the picture it provided of ordinary Zambwalians which was felt to be extremely flattering. The professor had found it very difficult to ascribe a plausible composite role to the African supporters of the revolt. Never having met any Zambwalians, apart from the waiters in the lakeshore hotel during his 1948 stopover, he had worried for some time over the problem of characterisation. Luckily, a summer vacation spent at his sister's cottage on the Gower peninsular and a couple of days in the Rhondda valley provided him with the answer. Zambwalians were delighted to find themselves described as hymn-singing, chapel-going, salt-of-the-earth socialists with powerful puritan traditions and long tribal memories. They were puzzled by the bit about them being passionate rugby fans, but the portrait as a whole was immensely reassuring and they were determined to live up to it.

The professor now crossed the senior common room with a smile which seemed to light up his thick spectacles, his right arm extending behind him as though trailing his unexpected African guest on a leash.

'Good evening, Vice Chancellor,' he declared loudly, using the title from necessity rather than policy since he never could remember the man's name. 'I want to introduce village headman Ngoleka.'

He turned to examine the end of the leash and found to comical bewilderment that his protégé had slipped his collar.

'Goodness,' he exclaimed. 'Well, well, I seem to have lost him.'

'Who is,' said the Vice Chancellor, 'or conversely who was, village headman Ngoleka?'

'Who was he?' Professor Lambkin was astounded when people failed to remember the details of his book. 'He was the boy hiding in the mango tree. He must be around here somewhere. Ah,' he added, identifying a probable culprit, 'Mackay.'

'I only took him for a quick drink,' said Mackay defensively.

Dr Mackay was senior librarian at the university. It was difficult to know whether he and Professor Lambkin were friends or enemies. In his days as librarian with the British Council, Mackay had supplied Professor Lambkin with much of the documentary evidence for his discussion of African attitudes to British rule in Zambwali—so much so that the professor had offered to dedicate the work 'To my dear friend Gordon Mackay who would have written a much better book'. Dr Mackay had modestly demurred and, his protest taken literally, the dedication had been withdrawn.

This had annoyed Mackay exceedingly. He had come to regard *Strike a Blow for Ethiopia* as his own book filched from him and given this ridiculous title. For many years, when on leave in Britain or attending library conferences in Africa or the United States, he had made it his business to inscribe the original dedication in every copy of Lambkin's 'little effort' he could track down.

'I only showed him where he could wet his whistle,' repeated Mackay aggressively.

'Where?'

'The bar, of course.'

The corner of the senior common room was fenced off with a counter. Four students were arguing angrily with the barman.

'He was there a moment ago,' said Mackay.

'How extraordinary,' said the Vice Chancellor. 'The case of the missing headman.'

He helped himself to a fifth sherry and motioned the waiter to serve the others.

'Sir,' said the waiter, offering the tray of drinks.

Professor Lambkin turned from his tiptoe survey of the room and accepted a sherry, frowning absent-mindedly at the waiter. Then he took a step backwards, horrified.

'Goodness,' he exploded. 'My dear fellow, what are you doing serving drinks?' He swivelled round. 'Mackay, this is quite outrageous.'

But Dr Mackay had already seized the tray and was verbally belabouring the barman, who protested in turn he thought village headman Ngoleka was one of the extra waiters.

'Pepani, sir, sorry, Truly, I did think he was a cleaner, sir. Pepani'.

The Vice Chancellor, as always, rose to the occasion.

'I've often wondered,' he said at his most charming, offering Ngoleka a glass of the South African sherry, 'I've frequently pondered whether when you were in the mango tree you could foresee what was to happen next?'

Village headman Ngoleka looked baffled.

'UM-TI WA MA-NGA' said Professor Lambkin, carefully differentiating his phonemes to make matters absolutely clear.

'Ndisaona kuti azungu asatimala,' said village headman Ngoleka at a furious pace. 'Ndisaona kuti asati namira ndi oyipa kwa ife akafiri osayuka. Asa kwata ziko yatu nbati patisa basa peze ndipo nbati pagarise nsongo. Awene asakala mbamwa pabodzi ndipo. Nkabe werenga Biblo. Ndisaona kuti awene ndi olamera mu ziko mwatu ndipo sa ziwa kulonga lingwa yatu. Penepi ndiye pina onene mu muti wa manga.'

Some of the nearby students guffawed and suppressed it quickly.

'Fascinating,' said the Vice Chancellor. 'Can anyone translate?'

'It seems,' said Lydia Hunter frowning, 'to be a rather unusual regional dialect.'

'I speak,' said village headman Ngoleka, 'but not good.'

He grimaced, and then explained.

'I see white people are finishing us off. I see they are cheaty and not kind to us poor blacks. They take our land and make us to work for nothing—peze peze—and they make us pay hut tax. They just sit and drink together and they do not read the true Bible. I see they are rich in our land and they do not speak our language. That is what I see in the tree of mangoes.'

'Extraordinary,' said the Vice Chancellor. 'But could you tell what was going to happen immediately afterwards?'

'I see all the white people are going to be killed'.

There was a sudden silence. One of the students tittered.

'In 1917, of course,' contributed Professor Lambkin helpfully,

'I do not say it in good English,' admitted village headman Ngoleka. Then, in a burst of inspiration, he added, 'We like white people come to Zambwali. We must help the Life-President develop the country.'

'Indeed we must,' said Professor Lambkin, putting his arm affectionately round his protégé's shoulders.

'Oh, yes,' said Lydia Hunter warmly.

'Quite,' said the Vice Chancellor.

Springer stared down at his new, highly polished toe caps, wondering about the plethora of voices.

That night, perspiring under his mosquito net, Springer had a nightmare. Precious, dressed in a school blazer and grey shorts and wearing his old prefect's badge, was dealing out punishments. One hour's detention after school on Thursday. The Vice Chancellor and he were to write out two hundred times, 'I will learn to be a good bwana.'

Suddenly, Precious was on a platform under a kachere tree, waving his fly whisk to the cheers of a huge crowd. He was making a speech and, as usual, his official interpreter was beside him. Translating everything he said into the local chi-Nyanja. Before him, in row upon row of semi-circles, sat thousands of members of the Women's Congress. Beyond, into the night, the crowds of villagers extended into infinity.

'Do you,' Precious shouted to the crowd, 'want to return to the stone age?'

His voice climbed in pitch and crescendo.

'Do you think an Africa could have invented the spinning jenny?'

The interpreter translated.

'Am I not a man and a brother? Is there not progress and development?'

'No,' roared the crowd.

Springer realised with a start the interpreter was Professor Lambkin and that both men were speaking in English.

'When I got my Mercedes-Benz,' roared Precious, 'when all Zambwalians get their Peugeot 404s, will you take them to an African to be repaired?'

Professor Lambkin interpreted.

'Are we not all members of the developed world? Does not the world spin for ever down the ringing groves of change?'

'No,' bellowed the crowd again and the Women's Congress ululated, ending in a prolonged wail.

Tossing and turning, Springer saw himself at the centre of an arena, dressed in a grass skirt and wearing amulets and anklets. He was supposed to be dancing. Women surrounded him in concentric circles, chanting a traditional praise song.

All things bright and beautiful,
All creatures great and small.

He had a python draped around his neck and in his right hand was a venomous black mamba. Dr Van Leiden was whispering in his ear, 'This is Chopa, the rain dance. You must compel the rains.' Somewhere a drum began beating. He moved round the arena, slowly, trying to match the beat, stamping with his bare feet and raising little spirals of dust.

The drum was joined by another, and then another, until a great battery of rhythm was driving him, as though his anklets were being tugged by a string held in the hands of the father drummer. The mamba had turned into a fly whisk and he had an axe in his left hand. The women were carrying green branches. Their singing urged him on.

The tall trees in the green wood,
The meadows where we play.

'You're not doing it properly,' said Dr Van Leiden. 'You're supposed to lead with the left. Put your left foot in, put your left foot out, put your left foot in, then shake it all about.'

'Conceptually,' Dr Lydia Hunter had said, 'conceptually their in the womb.'

She had brought in a script to be used in the GCE Human behaviour broadcasts, and he knew it was completely unsuitable, but his superiors were insisting he broadcast it. He was sweating in the studio because as soon as the microphone was on the air conditioning had to be switched off.

'Conceptually, they're in the womb,' he heard himself saying. His tongue was as dry as biltong. 'Consecutively, they're in the tomb. Contraceptively, this is a bomb. WHY DOES ZAMBWALI NEED EX-PATRIATES?' he shouted, turning to the script, trying to get his voice under control.

'There are more bwanas and donas in Zambwali today than ever in colonial times. Is it because the country can't manage without them? Is it because they perform jobs no Zambwalian is yet capable of doing? Is it because Britain makes it a condition of her aid programme that jobs should be given to the British? Is it because the Life-

President doesn't trust his own people and prefers to employs foreigners whom he can deport?

'Yes, of course, to all these explanations. But there is a further reason which must be explored through the discipline of social psychology. Put simply and without jargon, Zambwalians need expatriates as constant reminders of the colonialism they have repudiated.

'Our job, if we are to serve the country as it would wish, is to be arrogant not charming, greedy not generous, incompetent not effective, maintaining in our day to day behaviour everything British rule represented, so that each they kick one of us out they can re-visit the delirium of independence day. Our duty...'

A clatter of wooden spoons on saucepans woke him in a panic of perspiration. He sat up under the mosquito net, trying to work out where he was. This wasn't school camp. It was Precious, already in the kitchen at 5.00am., banging away at the overnight dishes.

This was too much.

'Shut up!' he bellowed.

'I haven't slept a wink all night,' he muttered to himself, padding along the passage.

'Shut up!' he shouted again, opening the passage door. Then added, in a barely audible whisper, 'you stupid kaffir.'

He shut the passage door and stood for a moment, trembling. Then, relishing the absolute silence, went back to bed.

In the kitchen, Precious shrugged his shoulders. If you're going to eat a frog, you might as well eat a fat one.

Suicide Bombers

I came to London to study film-making. I did literature and anthropology at the University of Zambwali, and it was Professor Hunter who fixed me up with a scholarship.

London was like being released from prison. It wasn't so much the girls—they were equally accessible back home and, in my view, back home they were prettier. No, it was the way you could talk, without worrying who was listening. Without checking who was behind the kitchen curtain, or lurking outside the window in the yard. The way books you knew only from the censorship list in the government gazette were openly on sale. And the newspapers. I've heard people say the British press is the worst in the world. But to read a variety of stories, all different from the one story allowed in Zambwali, that was paradise. And I dreamed of making my own stories and running my own film company.

Then—it was a condition of the scholarship—I went back to Zambwali, and was put in charge of the government film unit. My job was to film President Kacheche's speeches. My contract specified other duties, like promoting tourism and making documentaries. But the budget was small, and the speeches had to have priority, so there was never any money left for anything else.

A minimalist form, I called it in a letter I wrote to my college tutor. I never called it that again because I was summoned by the Soul Brothers (that's what we called Special Branch) to explain what I meant. But it was truly minimalist, with all the art in the editing.

At that time there were four cinemas in the whole country, three in the capital, one in the president's birthplace, plus a few halls where films were shown occasionally. Audiences were white, or coloured like Isabelinha (that's the mother of my children), or Indian like me. So the films were mostly for non-Africans and you had to bear that in mind. They were shown before the main feature, so I had fifteen minutes at most—otherwise, the audience just drifted off to the bar. A fifteen minute slice from a speech lasting up to four hours, beginning with Kacheche waving his flywhisk and ending with the national anthem. In practice, that gave me eleven minutes.

Some things were obvious. Always shoot from below, making Kacheche appear twice as tall as he really was. Always include the bit where he corrected his official interpreter, because Kacheche had forgotten most of his Nyanja and spoke in English, using an interpreter every three or four sentences. Rebuking the 'interrupter', as Isabelinha called him, for getting something wrong was part of the act. Always have a pan shot of the women in their various coloured clothes featuring Kacheche's smiling head, and be careful to make the crowd seem larger than it really was. The difficult bit was to figure out which eleven minutes of the four hours was official doctrine, and which just presidential rambling.

Obviously, it was not a job I was proud of. When my father saw one of my features he muttered it was worse than *Passion in the Jungle*. At the time, I didn't know what he meant.

Nor was it a job I could last long in. It was Banda at the ZBC tipped me off that I'd cut the wrong bit out of a speech about relations with South Africa. I crossed the river at dusk with only a suitcase, and got a London flight from Harare a week later.

I couldn't have done this without my father. Like all Indians, he'd managed over the years to get some money out. It was virtually an ethnic trait for Indians, and this capital got me started with my company, making films for television.

There's a problem with the medium, but at first it wasn't a problem. I wanted to tell stories, and it was a relief to get away from Kacheche's talking head and deal with real people and the events they were caught up in. I wanted to specialise in African stories. I couldn't go back to Zambwali, of course, that was far too dangerous, and I didn't want to do anything that would get my father or Isabelinha's family into trouble. But Africa's bigger than Zambwali. There were lots of countries that seemed pretty similar, and some a damn sight worse, and I had no history of trouble with any of them. So we filmed in Kenya and Nigeria and Chad, once even in Mugabe's Zimbabwe, and told good stories and made a living.

Most of them were historical. We did stuff about explorers—not Livingstone or Speke or Burton, but some of the more obscure ones like Young and Thompson and Phipson-Whybrants. Even now, you can sell these 'dark continent' stories. We did a super one about the African entrepreneurs at Zanzibar, the ones who put together the expeditions—people like Kiongwe and Bombay and Wellington, who used to meet the explorers and ask them where they wanted to discover and show them how to 'discover' it, only to be dismissed in the published accounts as rascally bearers and incompetent cooks. I even tried a half-hour piece on Henderson, my grandfather's lion-slaying hero. But it wasn't a success. Lion stalking wasn't easily reconstructed, not with our resources, and my baba wanted to talk the whole time and objected to anything he said being cut. I told him he was worse than Kacheche, but I was sorry I had said it because I love the old man and didn't want to hurt him.

And, of course, we did more up to date stuff, though those pieces were harder to raise a budget for and even harder to place in the schedules. Imperial nostalgia sells fairly easily, even nostalgia for Africa which hasn't the pulling power of the Raj. But stories of African resistance—for example, thirty minutes on the Mau Mau in Kenya—are still controversial, both on location when you're filming and in London when you're editing it for possible slots. Even today, there's an element of special pleading about such programs, and you easily lose your audience.

This is where the problem of the medium comes in. It's greedy for stories, and the stories have to be filmable. Images rather than words, action rather than description. That was more or less my creed, to find the image that is worth a thousand words. But story-telling makes the world coherent. It assigns roles, it builds shapes, it marks out boundaries. Who's in and who's out.

'Your grandfather was always full of stories.'

That was Isabelinha, my partner, trying for the hundredth time to be helpful.

My grandfather, Faruch. Yes, full of stories.

For the hundredth time, I tried to explain. 'When my baba came to Africa, he admired this Englishman you've heard him talk about, this Henderson Sahib. Then, when he realised Henderson was just a man like himself, he admired the Mahatma Ghandi. It wasn't his own story he was telling. He just had a small part in other people's stories. But he knew where he fitted in. That's what you and I don't know.'

'Don't we have a story?'

'Yes, of course we do. But what makes it interesting to anyone else?'

That thing about the image that says more than a thousand words. It was drummed into us at film school, and it was something I had to take seriously. I'm a Muslim, and as you know we're not supposed to deal in images. There's one of our proverbs—not the Koran, but in the Hadith which is supposed to be the sayings of Mohammed—that if you've been making images, when you get to paradise you'll be shown your images and challenged to bring them alive. If you can't do it, it's straight to hell for you. Allah's the creator, and you shouldn't try to beat him at his own game.

I'm not much of a Muslim, I even go to Mass sometimes with Isabelinha, but I like that story. Images are a serious matter.

But I've also come to believe something else: that images only work within cultures. Once you start showing things to people from somewhere else, you need words. Too many of them.

It's said that our story was about getting rid of Kacheche. The books are already appearing, on websites and from self publishers on *How We Overthrew the Tyrant.* I'm not denying some of these guys were incredibly brave. It took real courage for Charlie Mafambisse, the old paramount chief's son, to fly in from Addis Ababa and announce at the airport he was starting a new political party. Or Likambale Sisulu, printing his newspaper in Dar es Salaam and smuggling copies along the lakeshore by canoe. That was enough, in Kacheche's one-party state, to buy him a one-way ticket to Chiromo maximum security jail, where some people had been held for over twenty years.

The problem with the tale is that it's too simple-minded, another version of goodies and baddies, and how the goodies won. It simply repeats Kacheche's own story about how he overthrew British colonialism. But the questions swarm. How did he get away with it for so long? Why did we put up with twenty-seven years of tyranny? It's what my friends kept asking me in London. Why didn't you kick him out years ago if it turned out in the end to be so easy?

A man like me, son of a Muslim shopkeeper—because that's what my father was in the long run—has to start with the obvious. Ninety-five percent of Zambwalians are peasants, living for the most part on what they can grow in their own villages. A bit of maize or tobacco for the market, a lot of maize, sorghum, pigeon peas, groundnuts, pumpkins and sweet potatoes for surviving on throughout the year. This doesn't mean they're pig ignorant about politics. It just means they have a different kind of politics. They have their feet on the ground, which, let me tell you, is easier to do when you don't have shoes.

It was different in the 1960s when there was free education, and when a man could go to work in South Africa. Then, you could have a bit of ambition. Nowadays, the best you can hope for is that the rains come on time and your crops grow well and that there's peace in the country. That no one comes to steal your land, or that no refugees come and settle in your village.

That's what Kacheche delivered. Okay, he was a brute, a murderer, a cleptomaniac, a dictator with millions salted away in Switzerland. The man was quite frank about it. He used to boast he was the wealthiest man in Zambwali. They'd never seen palaces like his. The hospitals on his private tobacco estates were better than any government hospitals. When Lika Sisulu's newspaper started printing stories about all this, he wasn't saying anything Kacheche hadn't said himself.

But Kacheche gave the peasants what they needed most, just enough political stability for them to survive without any help from the state. Not all of them, of course, but enough of them. It was as though the state wasn't there. And, apart for tax collections and the thefts that always accompanied presidential visits, it wasn't there, and that suited them.

What changed? Well, two things. Zambwali didn't have much of a middle class, maybe two per cent of the population, but the population was growing and that two per cent became more numerous. There was a university, churning out graduates, like me and Isabelinha. We couldn't all join the regime, and we couldn't all be thrown to the crocodiles. And people like Likambale, who had been thrown to the crocodiles, or like Dr Kathupa, the heart specialist who was detained for wanting his operating room sterile, were suddenly martyrs. Dr Kathupa from the lakeshore had been trained in Germany, and the Germans didn't like to see their money wasted.

So the two per cent were free and active, founding newspapers and political parties, and the election came. And now they're all telling their stories of how they fought the regime. Even those who had been in exile all along, like me. As for the peasants, who cares about them any more?

These aren't the kind of stories I want to film.

We had a good life in London. I was doing a job I enjoyed, and was profitable. Isabelinha worked in a creche, so when the boys came we had no problem about baby-sitters. The colour thing never really bothered us. I always thought of it as a West Indian affair, people pushing for entry into English society exactly as the lower classes had done for generations, and being stupidly shut out. But that wasn't my ambition. I was born after independence, what Kacheche used to call 'the born frees' and I felt the Jamaicans in London had continued being colonised, obsessed with the class thing, long after the rest of the empire had gone its own way.

Something I grew up taking for granted—and again it's one of those things that takes a thousand words to explain—is how wide our circles were. I said I'm a Muslim of sorts, and Isabelinha's a Catholic. I also said Zambwali only had the tiniest middle class. There are educated Africans, of course, graduates from the university, or from Fort Hare in South Africa. Most of them are doctors or lawyers or teachers or civil servants. If you're an Indian like me you're in trade. The Hindus keep to themselves, with lives so private even fellow Indians aren't admitted. We Muslims are more outward looking. Our mosque has lots of African Muslims for Friday prayers. But our closest links, outside our own community, are with the mixed race people we call 'Coloureds'.

The Coloureds are the ones who keep things working. They own garages, they run transport companies, they fix typewriters and fax machines and now, of course, computers and mobile phones. Some of them, like the Rowlands, go right back to the beginning of colonialism, and they're very prominent. Most of them are Catholics. Some of them are rich.

Maybe because we're both small communities, there's a lot of inter-marriage between the Muslims and the Catholics. The rule is the girl takes the husband's religion. Muslim girls marrying Coloured boys become Catholic, and vice-versa. Isabelinha was supposed to have become a

Muslim when she married me, but I never insisted, and once we came to Britain it seemed pointless.

I say we're small communities, even in combination. But the families are enormous, and they spread far beyond the towns and far beyond Zambwali. We Muslims have big families, of course, but the Coloureds trump us in two ways. First, they're related to a lot of Africans. They're related to a lot of whites as well, of course, but the whites have never had much to do with them. I guess there must be Rowlands in England who have no idea they've got African relations. But the African links matter, especially when it comes to business deals and political protection.

Then, being Catholics, they've all got god-parents, who are almost as important to them as their blood relations. It's a kind of a supplementary family, just as extended as the real one. Isabelinha treats as 'family' people who turn up on our doorstep saying things like 'I'm your brother Ricardo's god-father's second-cousin'. That's his meal ticket for the next few days.

So all this means we know lots of people we regard as friends and family and half-family from all walks of life, as they say here—across religion, across the colour barrier, and pretty well anywhere where you want to go. If I have to go to Geneva, for example, or even San Francisco, there are doors I can knock on, just like Ricardo's god-father's second-cousin, and save a fortune in hotel bills.

I'm making a joke of it, but what it means is I've never felt in need of a nation. I never wanted to say I'm a Zambwalian, or my ancestors came from Bangladesh. My world was big enough already. I didn't even make much fuss about being a Muslim. But suddenly there's this roots business. Everyone's tracing their ancestors on the internet. I told Isabelinha, we used to laugh at the tribalists. All of a sudden, we have to join them.

And for me, as a Muslim, there's a new image. It's a child (because that's what they mostly are) with a Koran and a Kalashnikov and a green bandana round the forehead, videoed before setting off on his or her suicide mission. Explain that across the cultures. An honoured figure in Gaza, or parts of Leicester and North Finchley, feared and hated in Tel Aviv, and watched with baffled horror by Isabelhina and me. And I find, for the first time in my life, far more than in Kacheche's days, that I'm getting angry.

I had a friend at film school from Soweto in South Africa. He wore dreadlocks. In apartheid South Africa, this is going back to those days, his dreads were the sign he didn't belong to anyone, not a tribe, not a party, not a trade union, just himself with a passion for black American music. One day out of curiosity he went to the Rastafarian church in Brixton. He told me how weird it was—how he couldn't discuss with them a single African reality. It was all myth, and Ethiopia the biggest myth of all. Next week, he had his dreads cut off. I know now how he felt.

I don't argue with the fundamentalists, I don't issue fatwas, and I don't claim to be an expert on the Middle East. But I do know something about Africa, and the suicide bombers have planted this frustration in me of wanting to explain and explain and explain what Africa's about, and why everything I read in the press or see on television is wrong. I know how idiotic I sound, but the fact remains that my anger wants an outlet, saying, Look. Look at the facts.

Isabelinha hates it when she finds me shouting at some Irish nun who's been giving out bags of flour in the middle of some famine disaster and is appearing on

Newsnight, when I know there are a thousand African aid workers doing the real work behind the scenes.

'They have to show her,' she says, 'to raise the money.'

And I know, I know, but it's not enough. She hates it when I go crazy about the latest images of African babies with distended navels and flies crawling across their eyelids and no one brushing them away.

'They have to show them to raise the money.'

But what else are they showing—about feckless people who don't even understand their own world, and will always need kindly white folks to help them get by.

I long to make the film about Africa to end all films about Africa, and I've so many clips in my office, so many scribbled, incomplete scenarios.

*

EXT. AFRICAN TOWNSHIP

Wide-shot, mid-close-up gangs fighting, then zoom in on angry faces.

Confused shouting, sticks clash and some gunfire.

NARRATOR

Whenever fighting breaks out anywhere in Africa, journalists reach for the word 'tribe'. It's a comforting word. It means there are no issues, no land shortage, no unemployment, not even history as in Serbia or the Ukraine. Just primordial hatreds.

Cut-in dictionary, turn page, finger indicates word.

Background music. *I'm leaving on a jet plane.*

NARRATOR

The word next to 'tribe' in the Oxford English Dictionary is 'tribometer', an instrument used in physics for measuring friction.

INT. BEDROOM, MAN PACKING SUITCASE.

Mid-close-up.

Shouting, gunfire.

NARRATOR

The journalist is off to Luanda or Kinshasa to report on the latest troubles.

WOMAN'S VOICE

(Off-stage)

Have you packed your tribometer, darling?

Close-up man's amused face.

MAN

Of course, darling. I'd be lost without it.

*

EXT. VERANDAH OF AFRICAN HOUSE

Close-up blue eyes, blonde hair.
Background music.
Elgar's *Cockaigne Overture.*

NARRATOR

An Englishwoman, in her fifties, sun-scorched and dressed in khaki—

Mid-shot khaki shirt and shorts.
Rifle shots.

NARRATOR

firing round after round—

Close-up hand on rifle barrel, finger pulling trigger.

Fade out music/fade in Thomas Mapfumo's *Hokoyo*.

NARRATOR

across the veranda with its bamboo chairs and its cacti growing in milk tins, to protect the land her great-grandfather stole

Cut-in portrait

NARRATOR

from the great-grandfathers

Cut in portrait Lobengula.

Music increases in volume.

NARRATOR

of the veterans advancing with pangas to re-possess it.

Fade to gang advancing with pangas.

*

EXT. SWOLLEN RIVER, MOONLIT SURFACE.

Wide-shot pan slowly.

Soft timbila music.

NARRATOR

An American missionary, Southern Baptist, is secretly crossing the border.

Zoom in slowly on a dugout canoe with two paddlers.

Splashing sounds.

MALE AMERICAN

(Sotto-voce)

Their hearts are steady, they will not be afraid; in the end they will look in triumph on their foes.
Psalm 112, verse 8.

Mid-shot baseball-capped American seated in the stern.

NARRATOR

We are on the border between two African countries.

Cut-in map showing winding river border.

MALE AMERICAN

(Sotto-voce)

Be strong and bold; have no fear or dread of them, because it is the LORD your God who goes with you; he will not fail you or forsake you.
Deuteronomy 31, verse 6.

Mid-shot the paddlers turning to face current.

AMERICAN

(Excitedly)

It's the devil, come to block our mission.

Close-up of American

Loud splash and snort with snuffling sounds. American stands up in the dugout canoe, which rocks violently. American shouting and holding out a Bible in front of him.

AMERICAN

In the name of the Lord, be gone!

Hippopotamus surfaces with wide yawn, paddlers change course.

AMERICAN
(Normal voice)
He saved us, not because of any works of righteousness that we had done, but according to his mercy.
Titus 3, verse 5.

Mid-shot American standin in dugout, rocking violently

Snuffling and plopping sound.

NARRATOR
The missionary reports to his sponsors he found bodies in the bush, sure proof of 'terrorism'. His evidence, underlined in red in his report, is the encounter with the hippopotamus.

Close-up American holding bible before him. Wide-shot paddlers steadying canoe, American sitting.

Timbila music, rising and falling.

Mid-shot hippo submerges leaving tiny whirlpool. Wide-shot of river, canoe reaching far bank.

Soft timbilas.

*

INT HOSPITAL WARD, SOWETO.

Wide-shot of, pan slowly down right side, across end and up left side.

Background music. Miriam Makeba's *Uile ngoan 'a batho.*

NARRATOR

A maternity ward in Huntsville, near Soweto. Thirty beds crammed in a room meant for half that number, thirteen each side with two more at each end. Thirty young mothers, thirty new babies.

Cut music.

Zoom in on selected faces.

NARRATOR

But instead of laughter and gossip there's absolute silence in the ward.

Absolute silence.

NARRATOR

Even the babies are subdued.

Subdued but sharp drum rattle.

NARRATOR

Because every one of the mothers is HIV positive, and every new baby is infected.

Cut in to baby in cot, baby at breast. Pan slowly across beds and zoom out to wide-shot.

*

EXT. GROUP OF NYAO MASKED SPEAKERS.

NCHAWA MASK, FEATHERS, BENIGN RED FACE, SIGNIFYING ANCESTRAL SPIRITS.

Gule wamkulu drums, with the specific spirit drum rhythms: nchawa rhythm.

TALKING HEADS, NYAO MASKS

What does it mean to say a country's bankrupt? The point with bankruptcy is the creditors move in and take what they can lay their hands on. But you can't do that with a country. You can strip everything portable, like the Portuguese quitting Mozambique. But you can't come with wheelbarrows and carry away the soil.

LEBEDWE MASK, MONKEY FEATURES WITH LION SKIN, SIGNIFYING MISCHIEF.

Lebedwe rhythm.

TALKING HEADS, NYAO MASKS

First, government stops. Nothing official works. No schools, no hospitals, no electricity or piped water. No foreign exchange for imported necessities, like medicines or lorries.

NKHOKOMBA MASK, NGONI WARRIOR WITH OSTRICH SIGNIFYING BLOODSHED.

Nkhokomba rhythm.

TALKING HEADS, NYAO MASKS

For a decade, perhaps, there's an army, looting from people busy fending for themselves. Forget about government and nation, forget about education and development, just live as your ancestors did off the land.

CHEFU MASK, ELAND FEATURES; SIGNIFYING UNITY WITH ANIMAL KINGDOM.

Chefu rhythm.

TALKING HEADS, NYAO MASKS

The grandparents starve, the parents die of war or AIDS, and the children take to the path with their pangas.

TSEMPHO MASK, LEPROUS WOMAN, SIGNIFYING TERROR.

Tsempho rhythm.

TALKING HEADS, NYAO MASKS

From Mozambique to Sierra Leone, you could find them, armies of children on the march, inheriting nothing, fending for themselves by looting and killing.

Absolute silence.

TALKING HEADS, NYAO MASKS

That's when a country's bankrupt, when there's nothing left but children surviving by murder.

Subdued but sharp drum rattle.

*

These are a just a handful of the sequences I have in my studio as I have tried to piece together the film to end all films about Africa. It's difficult to keep up to date, so quickly do disasters accumulate. But the images are too simple. Stark, slap-in-the face, but saying at once both too much and too little. Requiring too much by way of voice-overs and talking heads to explain them.

The background to the maternity ward with its HIV babies is the long history of mining compounds in South Africa, with the sex lives of migrants limited to prostitutes or to each other. But another part of the background is the refusal of the ANC government to provide the drugs that might have saved the babies.

Or take those 'war veterans' attacking the white farms. They're far too young to have fought in the 1970s. Few of them can point to where their grandparents are buried. It so happens the woman they're attacking was one of the first whites to opt for Zimbabwean citizenship after independence. Her late husband was an actual war veteran, though not on Mugabe's side.

The stories are endlessly complicated, and the images don't join up—except at the level of the larger abstractions of, power versus powerlessness, exploiters versus the exploitable, rich versus poor.

So I opted to tell a different story, the one that moves me most. In a way, it's Isabelhina's story, but it's about more than just her and her background. It's the story I've almost finished narrating, starting off with Livingstone's funeral because that's where so much of it began, and ending with the tale that's coming. I couldn't have done it through images. I needed the forms in which people do a lot of explaining—letters, enquiries, diaries, interviews, and so on. I needed the occasions when people who wouldn't normally meet did so in face to face confrontation. In the end, it's the story that matters most. Oddly enough, now I've written it out, I think I can see how it might be treated.

Maria

It was in the gift shop at the Africa Centre in Covent Garden that I first saw one of Mavuso's pieces. A frog and a woman carved in ebony. I thought maybe it was meant to be the frog prince, just before the kiss, and it was only the technical cleverness that made me want to buy it. The two figures were interlocked—not coupling, just sort of bound up together—but they were separately moveable, which meant it had been carved from a single piece of wood. I couldn't really afford it—they wanted £120. But I'd just got my second-year student loan, so I blew a week's subsistence.

Back in Brighton I unpacked it in my bedsit. If the frog and the woman were lovers, had-been or would-be, I liked the way they were twined together but moved independently. But that's the trouble with African art. Your reasons for liking it turn out to have nothing to do with why you're supposed to like it. And I could see there were things I couldn't explain. The woman, for instance had what looked like a wooden nail hammered in, just above her right ear. I mean it was carved to look like that. But what did it mean? Did it symbolise subservience, so I was wrong about the independence? And the frog's front paws—why were they so large and expressive, like human hands?

I was curious. But I was behind with my assignments. I tried Mavuso on the internet, but it was a blank, a lot of Swazi princes and South African businessmen. So I left my frog and the princess on the sideboard and tried to forget how much I'd spent on it.

At Christmas, I went to my grandma's place in Ludlow. Jesus, it was cold and dull, and near impossible to get to without a car, but I'd promised and I had to deliver. I felt sorry for her, actually. She's a nice old lady, but she's been widowed since Dunkirk and her ideas about how 'young ladies' should behave seem to have died about the same time. She never got over my mother's divorce. It's supposed to be the children who feel these things, but she still goes on about it as though it happened yesterday. Not before I can remember.

On Boxing Day we took the bus to Church Stretton to visit a truly ancient lady she regards as a sort of great aunt. I don't think we're actually related, but when friends have been friends for long enough they become family. The story is her mother and my great-grandmother were close friends—close enough for there to be rumours about them. Especially after my great-grandmother left her husband, which wasn't easily done in those days. Anyway, as soon as I walked into the parlour, I saw it—a chair carved in ebony with six interlocking figures. Mavuso, I thought.

'That belonged to my mother,' said ancient Miss Haverstock. 'It was sent to her from Africa by your great-grandmother'.

'That long ago?' I exclaimed.

I'd been assuming Mavuso was a modern artist. Then I remembered they'd given me a certificate, Mavuso, Central Africa, c1923. That made him at least a hundred, if he was still alive. The chair was obviously much older. So he was working in an established style.

'I didn't know great grandma was in Africa,' I said.

'My dear girl,' said Miss Haverstock, 'You are an African yourself.'

So that was how I came to spend the end of 2002 pouring over Caroline's letters to Hortense, from the lady I thought was my great-grandmother to the lady who was Miss Haverstock's mother, learning about Asawilunda, about Peter and Paul and Daniel, about Charity and Emily, and about the brown girl called Maria who was sent to England and whose name is my own.

Miss Haverstock was an ancient lady and her malice passed me by completely. It was grandma who was upset for me and I realised I'd been taunted with what was supposed to be some kind of stigma.

Back in Brighton, I re-read the letters—I'd insisted on bringing them with me. Jesus, that was a different world! I began to see Miss Haverstock as someone whose life had been lived in the shadow of the rumours about her mother, and had maybe taken it out on little Maria. How did you explain a coloured child in Ludlow in those days?

I could see from the photos that Caroline had deceived herself, or perhaps Maria had changed as she grew up. In a checked frock for her tenth birthday, she looked unbearably fragile and pretty. But she could never have passed for white.

That January I spent a lot of time looking in the mirror.

Hair? Maybe. It was always springy. Nose? Perhaps. Lips? I like to think of them as generous. But they were the same old workaday features. When I compared them with the princess in Mavuso's carving, which was how I began to imagine Asawilunda, I couldn't see any connection. But Caroline had written she was no beauty, just a solid, immensely calm presence. Was that my inheritance?

I went back to my classes. I was a student. It was supposed to be all nurture, not nature. At least, as far as the University of Brighton was concerned.

Grandma didn't remember her mother. Maria had got married in 1916—Jesus, she was still a child—and was widowed within weeks at the Somme. Eight months later, she died in childbirth. Did Caroline weep for her? She had left Geoffrey by then, because he continued having children with various African women.

Did Miss Haverstock take on my grandma as a fresh cross to bear? Jesus, why were all these people so unkind?

I went for a long walk on Brighton beach, and relieved my feelings by chucking pebbles in the sea.

But of course, Caroline must have wept for Maria. She wasn't unkind. She was the one who had insisted something must be done for the children, however unpopular it made her.

I went back to my bedsit and read the final letters again. I could see that in combating the twenty-three wives—the aristocats, she called them—she had overlooked the shock to Ludlow.

Then it hit me. What about Peter, and Paul, and Daniel? They'd been sent to school in Portuguese Africa. Portuguese Africa? I couldn't even indicate that on the map. What had happened to them? Did they marry and have children, and grandchildren, and great-grandchildren like me? Was there a whole tribe—Jesus, what a word—a whole extended family of Clunies-Rowlands in Africa I was bound to and was completely ignorant about?

I decided I would have to go there. To Africa.

At first, it was no more precise than that. I had to go and find these people Caroline had written about. I took a couple of jobs, evenings and weekends. It meant my assignments suffered a little, but I went on getting pass grades and I reckoned I could make up when I got back. By June I'd cleared £2,000, and, with a month of full time work to follow, I could make my bookings.

Where to fly to? I felt I had two great-grandmas, one silent, one articulate, and Caroline's letters were my guide. I wished I could have followed her route, by liner to South Africa, steamer to Beira, coaster to Chinde, and paddle steamer up the Zambesi. She wrote about drifting days at a time down a winding, green river with many channels, unable to see beyond the plumed reeds and exploding heads of papyrus. I explored this same route upstream on the map, and the more I thought about it, the more confused I became.

What made her journey possible in a region ravaged by wars? Wasn't it colonialism, which had brought a bit of order? Now I wanted to make the same journey, up a river ravaged by similar wars. But colonialism was one of my taboos.

Naturally, I had to go by plane, but it made me think. I went back down to the beach, along there by the pier, and flung a few more pebbles into the channel. Then I decided that how I got there was irrelevant, what mattered was I should go.

The internet isn't actually very useful in cases like this. I found out there was an Alexander Clunies-Rowland who served as a private in the American war of independence, which was interesting but not to the purpose. I also contacted a Sergeant Clunies-Rowland in Pretoria. He had some distant connection with Geoffrey, but cut the connection at the idea that he might be part black.

There was a heady moment when one of my fellow students told me about the ancestor's project in Salt Lake City—how the Mormons had computerised birth registers world wide so the pious could pray their ancestors into heaven. At a price, of course. Prayers like that cost money. Then I remembered Caroline saying these births weren't registered. 'The great empire on which the sun never set' etc. She had a mind of her own, that lady.

In the end, I booked to Bangwe, just two flights a week via Harare and horribly expensive. I left on August 3rd, the height of the cold season, and in every way unprepared.

What came next sounds a bit like the Perils of Pauline. I wish it didn't because I'd truly like to be heroic.

The airline had booked me into a hotel. It was necessary to have a destination, they said, to get into the country. But all I really wanted was a cheap room for a few weeks. I mentioned this to the passenger sitting next to me, a nurse from the city hospital. When we arrived, just after dawn, she told her brother, who had come to meet her. I was struggling with the forms. Was I a tourist? Yes, of course. Where was I going to stay? I wrote the name of the hotel. Race?

What was my race? I thought about Mongoloid, Negroid, Caucasian. After much hesitation, I wrote Caucasian and presented the form to the officer at the immigration desk.

'What's this Caucasian? Are you European, coloured or black?'

'Coloured' I ticked, and was rewarded with a funny, official look.

'Faith say you need a room?' said an African at my elbow.

'Faith?'

'My sister.'

I turned, and saw my fellow passenger.

'We have room,' he said.

He grabbed my suitcase and I followed them both to the car park. Jesus, his car looked older than me. He flung my suitcase on top, and flung open a door hanging on its hinges. When I hesitated, he grabbed my arm and propelled me into the front seat.

'Let's go,' he said.

So there I was, in Africa.

My first impression was it was damned bumpy. My next was that we were climbing on a switchback road, not just up and down but sideways, between tin-roofed shanties with adverts for laxatives and kidney-pills. It looked dry. There were mud houses with untrimmed grass roofs, and beyond them hills crowned with speckled boulders. It didn't feel like a place with a destination. Then we drove under a plywood arch, decorated with cockerels proclaiming 'National Independence' and we were in the capital city.

'I bring you this way to show you the sights,' said my fellow passenger's brother. 'Now we go home.'

He swung the wheel violently and we climbed a steep hill lined with Indian shops and bottle stores, then round something he said was the parliament building, then down a tree-lined avenue and into the grounds of a large wooden bungalow.

Jesus, I thought, could this be Caroline's old house?

In the end I found it wasn't, but it could easily have been hers because they were all so alike, with wide verandas and polished stone floors, glassy with age. We sat on bamboo chairs and drank locally brewed Carlsberg beer, looking out across a wide plain with a silver winding river and I wondered if anything had really changed.

That night, Faith's brother came into my bedroom and tried to rape me. I don't know why he needed to do that, or what exactly it had to do with Asawilunda and all those other women. Luckily, I got my right arm free and attacked his eyes. When we both screamed and Faith rushed into the room, he gave up and stormed off in a furious temper. Poor Faith was so upset I ended up being the one comforting her. But of course, I couldn't stay longer in that house.

The Zambwali telephone directory is a brown notebook —at least, the thirty-year old edition I found in the bedroom corner when I got up before dawn to escape. I walked with my backpack along the avenue and down the hill past the parliament building and the Indian shops to the main road. Unlike Brighton and despite the twilight, everyone was already on the move. There was a newsagent open and a bar with tables outside. People were drinking pale sugary tea and eating sandwiches with fillings of French fries. I asked for a coffee which turned out to be instant and made with condensed milk but, Jesus, I needed something consoling.

Afterwards, I realised I could have done all this much more straightforwardly. If I'd taken a taxi from the airport to the main hotel in Bangwe, I wouldn't have been attacked and I'd have found an up to date directory in my bedroom. Except that would have got me nowhere. The one I was studying as I drank my coffee was heavily inked on coarse paper and included numbers like Monkey Bay 1, alongside adverts for hair straighteners and skin lightning creams. But nothing was listed for anyone called Clunies-Roland.

'Madam, what are you troubling yourself for with that old book? Don't you know basically this is a modern country? We have internet and mobile phones.'

It was the Indian boy who had brought my coffee.

'The people I'm looking for are probably dead by now. But I'd love another coffee. Do you have real milk?'

'We have proper local coffee. You only had to ask. Basically, most people want imported.'

'And a toasted cheese sandwich?'

'I will bring it.'

I don't know what I expected to find in Africa. Jungle? Of course, I knew better than that. Giraffes walking down the main street? What surprised me was it was all so like Brighton, except all happening three hours earlier than there. In Brighton, only office cleaners were on the move this early. But these people queuing for taxis looked like professionals.

The sandwich was good and the coffee deserved a different name from what I was served first.

'If you are looking for someone dead, my Bap knew all those old Europeans.'

'Bap?'

'My grandpa. Father's father. He in the back shop. Come and ask him'

I followed him past the counter, past a woman in a sari sitting at a huge cash register, though a low doorway and into the kitchen, and on again through another low door into a warehouse with shelves each side packed with bolts of cloth.

'This is Bap's business. I just run the café.'

We stepped out into the sunlight at the back into—well, into what? It wasn't a yard because it wasn't paved, and it wasn't a garden because nothing was planted there. It was just scraped hard earth that looked as though it had been freshly swept, and there was an old tree in the corner. A hammock was slung between the tree and a hook in the corner of the house, and an old Indian man in a string vest and trousers was rocking gently.

'Bap? This madam—sorry madam, I don't know your name—'

'Maria.'

'Miss Maria, Bap. She is trying to trace some people. I told her you knew all the old Europeans.'

The old man sat up awkwardly, his bare feet dangling.

'It true,' he said. 'I knew many people. But my father—he is long dead—he knew everybody in the colony. He was with Henderson Sahib. You hear of him?

'I'm afraid not. But the people I'm looking for—'

'Henderson Sahib, he killed the lions. When they were building the railway. Roshan, go get the book.'

The Indian boy darted off.

'My father plant this mango tree when he bring my mother here from India. My mother, Muhsin. She was frighten to come here because she thought she would miss her mangoes. So he planted this tree for her. Then she died, when I was born. So I never knew her, I just have this tree.'

Roshan returned with a dusty covered book he was busy polishing on his shirt sleeve. He gave it to the old man who passed it on to me. I read the title, *Passion in the Jungle* by Cynthia Springer.

'It supposed to be about Henderson Sahib. My father is supposed to be in it. Gun bearer. But he hated the book. He said it was all nonsense and it made him angry'.

Roshan intervened.

'What is the name of the people you are looking for?'

'Clunies-Roland,' I said. 'That's the family name. But the old men must be dead by now'.

'Clu—what?'

'Clunies-Roland. But they are not Europeans. They are coloureds, like me.'

The old man stared at me intently.

'You is a coloured?' he said, surprised. 'I could usually tell, but with you—'

'My great-grandmother was the sister of the people I am looking for. There was Peter Clunies Roland, then Paul, and then Daniel.'

'Ah!'

The old man´s gums gaped in triumph.

'Mr Rowland! The politician. He had that farm just down there on the Lichinga road.'

Rowland? I thumbed the old directory and there were the names. Rowland, Peter; Rowland Paul. No Daniel.'

'I never hear of Mr Daniel, and Mr Paul died Portuguese side long time back. But Mr Peter, he used to be customer at my shop. His daughter marry Dos Santos, who own the wine shop. He is dead but she still living.'

'Then she is my aunt,' I said. 'Or my great-aunt.'

A week later, I still had the feeling that I was missing out on Africa. It was odd in ways I couldn't quite pin down.

The house I was living in belonged to old Mrs Dos Santos, Peter's widow, but it was rented for practically nothing by her grandson Pedrinho—that's 'little Peter', a huge man with a paunch, and his wife Fatima. We worked out one evening they're my cousins twice removed, though they don't call it that here. They just run through the list of all the people that intervene between you and them, and when the string is complete —it usually takes about twenty minutes to get everyone in—they give you a hug and treat you ever afterwards like close family.

The routine was like this. Every morning just after seven, Pedrinho, Fatima and the three children, Teresa, Paulo and Ito (short for Carlito) left the house in the Range Rover. Pedrinho owned a transport business with a huge garage where Fatima kept her own car. She then drove Teresa and Paulo to primary school, and dropped off Ito at the crèche, before continuing to the solicitor's office where she worked as a secretary.

As soon as they all left, the servants moved from their quarters at the bottom of the garden into the main house. It wasn't just Pedrinho and Fatima's house where this happened—the whole estate was the same, big houses inhabited by the owners at night and from Saturday lunchtime to Monday morning, and by their African servants the rest of the time. When I joked to Fatima about how strange it seemed, she looked puzzled at first, then said it the best way to keep out thieves. It was cheaper than getting a security guard and you couldn't rely just on dogs and alarms. That was why she kept her car at her husband's garage. After that conversation, I walked round the garden and realised I was living in a fortress, with huge metal fencing topping with electrified barbed wire. What did that tell me about Africa?

The first morning I was left alone with the servants, I felt very out of place. They took over the kitchen, the living room, all the bedrooms with their separate bathrooms, and it was obvious they felt the house was theirs for the day time and that I was an intruder. I had to sit on the veranda to be out of their way, with Fatima's photograph albums to keep me company.

These were fascinating—her own and her sisters' weddings, christenings with the boys like Little Lord Fauntelroy and the girls sugar plum fairies, Paulinho's father's and mother's wedding (with his mother obviously near her time) and then Peter, my uncle, sitting in a deck chair with a very young Mrs Dos Santos in the group standing behind. Everything was terribly formal, and there were no holiday snaps. No one having fun at all, until towards the back there were sloppily dressed Europeans with solar topees, standing beside ancient cars or leopards they had shot. Right at the back was Caroline in a white calico dress and cork hat. Geoffrey's photos, though, were macabre. He was pictured in bed reading a letter from one of his sons, in a coffin surrounded by flowers, six foot down in the earth, and then buried under a heap of earth and more flowers. All this, the caption said, in Bristol, and it raised a question in my mind. Who sent so it could end up in Fatima's album?

But I also noticed that going back through the generations—Pedrinhos's father, then Peter, then of course Geoffrey and Caroline—the faces got whiter. There were no African faces and no picture of Asawilunda.

This occupied me for an hour or so. What next? Then I thought, Jesus, this is too ridiculous, and I went back to the kitchen to make some coffee and try to talk to the servants. They were very suspicious at first, like I'd been left behind to spy on them. But then I asked them what was their word for bread and milk and how to say thank you, and they started giggling at my accent. I laughed back and asked 'How you do say sorry?' and they said 'Pepani, madam'. I replied 'Pepani, madam' and that made them laugh all the more, and after that we started to become friends. It was much easier than when Caroline went visiting the servants in the lines and came back saying it was like Lady Bountiful visiting the peasants, because in a strange way I was on their territory and they were the hosts. Also I didn't have a distance to maintain, as she did because of the twenty-three wives.

Malotta I especially liked. She was no older than me but she already had three children by a husband who'd gone to study medicine in Edinburgh and got married there to someone called Macintosh.

'How could he do that?'

'Oh, mine wasn't a court wedding with papers and things. We just did it in the village'

She asked me if Macintosh wasn't the same as a raincoat. When I agreed, she giggled and said it was like marrying an umbrella. What struck me was she didn't much mind. Having three children was much more important than having a husband. Her mother in the township looked after them while she was at work, and she saw them only on Sundays. The oldest was six and still not in school. In fact, when I questioned more closely, it was obvious none of them would ever go to school unless Pedrinho or Fatima paid. Her wages would never cover the school fees.

I asked Malotta about Mavuso, the carver. She knew several Mavusos, so it took some time to establish she couldn't help me. Actually, this was interesting, though I didn't know it at the time. When I checked at the national museum, they knew Mavuso there, and were very excited I had a carving of his. Those who could afford his work knew him. It was ordinary Zambwalians like Malotta who'd never heard of him. Or perhaps forgotten him.

But she knew the story about frog and frog's wife. She giggled when I asked her about it and said it was just something silly from the bush. Only when it was clear I wouldn't stop nagging her about it, she sat down on the kitchen chair with a bowl and some potatoes to peal, and told me.

There was a Frog who, yes, like madam said, was a carver. He had two friends and the three of them always did everything together. If they went to cut poles or grass for their houses, they came home with their bundles and the first friend sang:

> *Wife of Johnson,*
> *Help me,*
> *Help me unload this bundle*

The second friend sang

> *Wife of Mbuza*
> *Help me,*
> *Help me unload this bundle*

But frog could only sing

> *Mother of Frog,*
> *Help me,*
> *Help me unload this bundle*

And the friends would laugh at him because he didn't have a wife.

One day, Frog went into the forest and stayed there a long time. From the heart of an ebony tree, he carved a woman, smooth and black with shining breasts and buttocks. Then he stuck a pin in her head to turn her into a human being, and secretly married her. Next time the three friends went foraging, and they came back, frog was able to sing

Wife of Frog,
Help me,
Help me unload this bundle

and the two friends were astonished by the woman's beauty. They were so impressed they couldn't keep the secret to themselves and eventually the chief came to hear of this beautiful wife of Frog's. He resolved to have her for himself and sent his soldiers to kidnap her and bring her to his palace.

But Fly saw what was happening and hurried to warn Frog. Then Frog called on all his friends in the forest to help rescue Beauty. Dove agreed to sing her most melodious song. Hawk agreed to be ready to pounce. All the other birds and animals marched on the chief's palace. The chief came out onto his veranda to investigate the commotion and Dove sang her most melodious song. So the chief invited Beauty to join him on the veranda to hear the music and, as she emerged from the palace, Hawk swooped down like lightening and drew the pin from Beauty's head. She became just a piece of wood once again.

So, I thought. That explains Mavuso's piece. Now all I had to do was figure out what the story meant. Malotta caught the frown crossing my face and immediately apologised.

'I did tell you, madam, it was just something silly from the village.'

'No, no. It was exactly what I wanted to hear. But isn't Frog just back to square one?'

'Madam, what is one square?'

It was Malotta's turn to pull a face.

'I mean he's back to not having a wife.'

'It could seem that way.'

She giggled again, but I couldn't get her to discuss the matter. She washed the potatoes and threw away the peel, and got on with other tasks.

The story nagged me. After all, it was where I'd started, buying Mavuso's carving with my student loan. Already, it had brought consequences, Jesus, hadn't it just.

But, surely, Frog was back to square one. Or was he? Was outwitting the chief the real point of the story? Could he now take his chunk of ebony home and turn it back into a wife to help unload his bundles? Why did she have to be beautiful to do that? And what of Beauty's part in all this, the silent woman passed from hand to hand? Mightn't she have preferred to live in the chief's palace rather than be the wife of a clammy frog? Ugh.

That's how we we'd have discussed it at the University of Brighton, deconstructing it in terms of class and gender—race too, I suppose, if the animals were taken to be a different group. But that wasn't going to work here. I knew I was missing something.

By now, of course, I knew I was living in a compound. I'd expected an ocean of connections and ended up like Caroline, impatient with her aristocats.

Admittedly, there seemed to be no end of people I was related to, and no end to their hospitality. Wives would pick me up each morning and drop me off when they collected their children from school. Weekends, despite the season—it was actually quite cold this time of the year, and we had log fires at night—the men organised lavish barbecues, or bries as they called them, involving a dozen families, each playing host in turn. The steaks were good and the drinking was on an epic scale. I couldn't believe how many empties were put aside to be thrown away next morning.

I gave up trying to keep track of who was who. Most of them seemed to be connected in some way with the original Peter Clunies-Rowland, as I still called my great-uncle. But since he had had three wives and, like his father, other women on the sly, he left a lot of descendents. Paul, who had died in Mozambique, had also left children, and some of their children had come back to work in Zambwali, running away from the war. Or they had married Zambwalian men. Nobody knew anything about Daniel who must have died a long time ago.

Then, of course, there were the wives' families, with lines stretching almost to infinity. Beyond that they all had godparents whose families seemed equally part of the scene. Some of them, and this surprised me, were Muslims. They intermarried with that community under some rule that the girls adopted their husbands' religion. I have to say it didn't stop the men drinking.

At first, I tried making lists of the people I'd met, or been to lunch with. But I decided in the end it didn't matter. No one seemed to bother too much about anyone's credentials, and I got the impression anyone could turn up if they drove a big enough car.

Despite having a career of her own in the solicitor's office, Fatima was incredibly housebound. She never discussed her boss or her colleagues. She was a little mouse of a woman with wide-spaced, easily frightened eyes, and never happier than when running a duster over the TV or the HI-FI, even when Malotta had left them spotless.

I soon realised she was terrified of Africans. Even the servants made her nervous, and Malotta with her giggling was 'too cheeky'. She said this when I raised the question of Malotta's children. 'Those people don't need educating,' she said. Those weren't her precise words, but if I repeat exactly what she said it would make her sound malicious, and she wasn't in the least. She was just living in the little world of her group.

There was only one African for whom she had unstinting praise, and that was President Mafambisse, whose framed photograph she had in her kitchen, and who alone knew how to keep people in their proper places. Otherwise, the high security fence with its electrified barbed wire kept out another world of thieves and predators.

But she had a deeper anxiety. I could see it in those wide brown eyes every time Pedrinho parked in the gravel drive after a night's drinking in the township bars. Worse than thieves, there was disease out there. It had already affected families she was linked with, and it might at any moment infiltrate the metal gates.

Suddenly, one Tuesday afternoon, all this changed. Pedrinho arrived much earlier than normal, with Fatima and the children in the Range Rover. Old Mrs Dos Santos was sitting in the back.

'Tia Helena's dying,' he announced abruptly. 'Pack your things. And bring your passport.'

'Where are we going?' I asked Fatima.

'Chinde,' she said. 'Portuguese side.'

It took me five minutes to put together my backpack, and I sat in the Range Rover with Mrs Dos Santos while Pedrinho paced up and down the lawn, talking into his mobile phone.

'Dona Helena,' said Mrs Dos Santos, 'is my mother.'

I tried to work this out. Jesus, this went back four generations.

'Not my real mother. She is my father's first wife.'

'How old is the old lady?'

'We don't know for sure. I'm going to be eighty in November. Dona Helena must be over a hundred.'

The rest was bustle, an emergency security guard for the house, and we were off, hurtling east into the gathering dusk.

At the border we joined a queue of cars, travelling in convoy to the same destination. Pedrinho took our passports to the immigration post and returned with bad news. The old lady had passed away.

'Ah, Santa Maria,' muttered Mrs Dos Santos, and crossed herself.

It was a long drive through the night down what had once been a highway but was reverting to dirt, with tyre-slashing ridges of tarmac lining deep gullies. For once, the Range Rover was serving its purpose. We stopped at Mocuba where someone had telephoned ahead to the restaurant bar that a large party was coming, and over rotary chicken and cold chips I saw our fellow travellers. Most of them I knew, from the various barbeques, but there were African faces I hadn't encountered.

It was almost dawn when Pedrinho parked in a clearing fringed by coconut palms and we stretched our legs in the cool air. Before us, pewter coloured in the dim light was a wide, fast-flowing river. Mosquitoes, neutered by the cold, drifted like a drizzle in the light breeze. The children wanted to pee and I helped Fatima by looking after little Ito.

Cars kept arriving and parking—by now there were well over a hundred of us, including lots of faces new to me.

'Where's Chinde?' I asked Pedrinho.

'Other side,' he said. 'We can cross here by motor boat, or drive upriver to the pontoon.'

I stared across at the fringe of coconut palms, like black lace against the sunrise. The men were conferring.

The boat crossing was the simplest option, though it would take about ten trips to get everyone across. But that meant abandoning the cars in the bush with no one to guard them. The pontoon was agreed on.

Once again, we piled into the cars, winding in procession down a narrow track along the riverbank under the coconut palms and an occasional grove of mango trees.. There came a point where the river, gleaming gold now in the sunlight, divided either side of an island, and it was here we crossed on a motor driven pontoon, its sides boarded up with plywood and bits of canvass. It could only take three cars at a time, but we were in the first group and we drove on without waiting for the others.

The old lady's wake lasted seven days and seven nights and, though it seems a strange thing to say about a funeral, I've never felt so fulfilled in my life.

By the time we reached the sprawling wooden house, Dona Helena had been dead some fourteen hours. While we were driving through the night, her family and friends had sat beside her, for the dead are not to be left alone. We filed passed her coffin, and I stared down at a tiny wizened face, leathery as a turtle's, with wisps of white hair around her skull. Then we embraced an old African lady I later learned was Dona Helena's sister, and the press behind pushed us out into the hot sandy courtyard milling with, Jesus, I couldn't count how many people.

I remembered the immigration officer asking me at the airport, 'What's this Caucasian? Are you white, coloured or black?' and it struck me, all that's irrelevant here. The blacks outnumbered the coloureds and we coloureds outnumbered the whites and Indians, but so what? We were all there to mourn a lady and 'keep warm' the bereaved.

Those words were Mrs Dos Santos's, and I loved her for them. We were to stay, all four hundred or so of us, in that house and courtyard until the seventh day mass so the people left behind could be comforted. Jesus, where was everyone going to sleep? How were we going to be fed? But it all worked out.

The priest came late afternoon, just after candles had been lit at the head and foot of the coffin. There was a brief mass, and then a procession to the cemetery outside the town at what I later learned was the highest point in Chinde, just fifteen feet about sea level. As the old lady was lowered into the sand, we filed past throwing handfuls of sand on to the coffin. It was brief and simple, and by dusk it was done.

I ate what I was given, not knowing how to help prepare it, and I slept in a cupboard allotted to me by Dona Helena's sister, who knew me as the English girl and an unknown quantity. She gave me a sleeping mat and a piece of mosquito netting to cover the ventilation panel, and I slept like a brick.

Next morning, I faced my first real challenge. I was up at dawn and was shown the pit latrine and a little square surrounded by sacking where I could shower with a bucket of water from the pump and a tin mug. As I came out into the sandy courtyard, I heard a chopping sound. Two men were holding a cow's head by the horns while a third was using a machete to cut a v shape in its forehead. I shuddered as he stuck the machete inside and drew out a chunk of the brain which he passed to some old women sitting by a cooking fire. They put it directly into a large frying pan where some eggs were also sizzling, then offered me a portion of both on a metal plate along with a fork. My gorge rose when I tried them, but the 'miolos', as they called them, tasted fantastic and I had a second helping. After that, I felt ready for anything.

I noticed most of the men had gone off on various bits of business, but they all returned in the afternoon bringing tins and sacks of supplies, along with crates of beer and bags of charcoal. During the day, every day, the women sat on the sand in groups, making preparations for the evening, and I wandered among them, leaving Fatima and the children with Mrs Dos Santos in the wooden house.

There were women pounding maize in a huge ebony mortar, two at a time with six foot pestles keeping up a steady rhythm. I tried to have a go but only succeeded in making them crease with laughter. Jesus, that pole was heavy and I couldn't get the rhythm, jerking my body up and down, so my pestle kept colliding with the other lady's. Since she had a baby on her back, I could only shake my head in shame at failing to do something every woman should be able to do.

It was the same with plucking chickens. They were amazed I'd never done it, and wondered if we had chickens in England. One lady had worked for a sugar company upriver and spoke a little English to supplement the words I'd learned from Malotta, so we sorted that out. But my hands weren't strong enough to pull out wing feathers and again I gave up. At last, where one lady was shredding coconuts, I found something I could do. She showed me how to drain the milk and then bang the end with a mallet and pin so it fell into portions. I sat astride a stool that had a serrated metal tongue at one end, and dragged the pieces of shell across it to the shredded flesh fell into a bowl. I could do that all day, and spent several days preparing the coconut for use in the chicken and goat stews.

By lunchtime, I had discovered something new. It was far more important to taste people's food than to have shared in preparing it. Then, after a siesta in the black shadow of a mango tree because, Jesus, it was hot down here, I had a big surprise.

'Miss Maria, I am surprised to see you here.'

I sat up suddenly, squinting in the brightness. It was the Indian boy from Bangwe who served me coffee the morning after, whose grandfather told me about the Rowlands.

'Roshan, I'm surprised to see you here. Are we related like everyone else?'

'I think one of my aunties married one of your uncles, or something. I would need my computer to work it out.'

He frowned at the thought and added, 'Even then, I'd need special software.'

'Is your Bap here?'

'He is not well. I am his representative.'

'What's wrong with him?'

'Basically, he is old.'

He asked me if I'd seen the town.

'Only the cemetery.'

'I will show you. It is different from Bangwe.'

We left the sand behind for another of those stretches of potholed tarmac we'd bumped over on the way down. There was about half a kilometre of dual carriageway with a line of concrete street lamps in the middle, and we walked up one side and down the other. One side of the road was a school, a church, a town hall, a police post, a square than had once been a park a football club, and some offices, while the other side was a line of bungalows.

'Where's the hotel" I asked, remembering Caroline's first letter.

'What hotel?'

'The famous Murray's.'

'I did never hear of any Murray.'

'But the English section. There was an English colony here.'

'That is basically in the sand part. All that bush where we are staying.'

I resolved to explore further. Tomorrow, when I'd done my chore with the coconuts. As we returned past the school to the wooden house, Roshan asked me if I'd heard of his uncle.

'He is a film producer. He lives in London. He is called Rashid.'

'What kind of films does he make?'

'Oh, about David Livingstone. And one about man-eating lions. He is always on your television.'

'I hardly watch television.'

'Perhaps he could make a film about you, coming to Bangwe to find your family. Then he would have to film you meeting me, and basically I would be famous.'

I was careful not to smile.

Back at the house I sat on the wide veranda with Mrs Dos Santos and told her I'd been to see the town, walking up and down the main street.

'In the old days,' she said, 'the Portuguese used do that every Sunday afternoon.'

'What? Just back and forwards?'

'In their best clothes. Even the children. Some of them used to drive their cars round and round. But Chinde is finished.'

I remember the phrase in Caroline's letter, 'Chinde's best days are over.' This was a place of strange ghosts.

Next morning while I was sitting astride the stool grating coconuts, Dona Helena's sister came to squat beside me on the sand. She was a tall, rather masculine woman with skin like ebony and a comb stuck in her close cropped hair. She was smoking a home-made cigar by putting the lighted end in her mouth and blowing on it before inhaling the smoke. To my surprise, she spoke very good English.

'I have been watching you,' she began. 'You are a very good girl.'

I had the sense not to reply.

'They say Senhor Pedro is your uncle.'

'My great-uncle, yes.'

She blew again on her cigar and I worried for her throat.

'I do not understand how.'

'Mr Peter had a sister. When his father's English wife sent Mr Peter and Mr Paul and Mr Daniel to school this side, she sent the daughter to England.'

'I never heard tell of that. What was her name?'

'Maria, same as me. She married an Englishman who was killed in the Great War. Soon after, she died, giving birth to my grandmother. I didn't know this. I only found out last Christmas. So I decided to come to Africa to find my family.'

'Ha,' she exclaimed. 'And have you found them?'

'I don't know. I've met a lot of people with the same name. But they don't feel like family. I've more in common with my friends in England.'

There, I'd said it. I hoped I hadn't offended her.

'You are a good girl,' she repeated. In one swift movement, she stood up and strode away. I went on grating coconuts.

That afternoon, she woke me from my siesta under the mango tree. She was accompanied by an old man, very black, very frail, with an elaborate carved fly whisk. For a panicky moment I wondered if he was some kind of witchdoctor. Before she squatted beside me, she ordered one of the women to bring the old man a chair. She took her time, rolling and lighting up a fresh cigar which she smoked in the same way, putting the lighted end in her mouth and puffing her cheeks as she blew on it. She made me nervous. I could see people were moving closer to overhear what she had to say to me.

'My mother, Sinhala Patience, used to say there are two kinds of families. There is the British type of family, and there is the kind of family we Africans know.'

There were whispers in the audience, then a hum of approval as these words were translated.

'How she knew,' the old lady continued, 'was because she was married to a White Man.'

This time the hum was one of surprise.

'His name was Mister Thomas. He belonged to the mission. Right there in Migodo.'

She waved the cigar vaguely to the north.

'Bwana Tomasi Smart,' said the old man unexpectedly.

'He was not my father. After he died, my mother Sinhala Patience, she married my real father Ngoleka. But because of her first husband, she made me learn English. Right there in the old school in Bangwe.'

Once again, she took a long pause, puffing theatrically.

'Two kinds of families. The British type, and the family we Africans know. The British type is for men. The man says, my wife, my sons, my house, my land. My wife lives with me, I choose who my daughters marry, I decide what is to be planted in my shamba. That is how Mr Thomas used to talk. And Sinhala Patience used to say, Mr Thomas is a good man, he treats her very kind, but that is not a marriage. That is Ngoni marriage, that is slavery.'

I remembered Caroline's letter about Geoffrey granting all those divorces.

'Sinhala Patience said, tribes are for men, families are for women.'

People clapped at this. Even the old men seemed to approve, and I had a sudden vision of families traced through the female line and spreading everywhere through the women's genes. Jesus, I thought. How many people are we talking about? In how many places?

'Your Anganga,' the old lady continued.

'Asawilunda,' I said.

'You already know that?'

'It is what I found out last Christmas.'

'After Mister Geoffrey went away and her children were taken, your Anganga married again. Like Sinhala Patience. She became Chief Nazombe's wife. This man is Chief Nazombe's grandson, the present chief. He is your oldest living relative.'

I had seen enough to know what I had to do. I knelt on the sand before the old man with my head bowed and my fingertips pressed together.

'Filha,' he said, laying his hand on my head. 'My daughter.'

Afterwards, I took the walk I'd planned, following a sand track past Dona Helena's into what looked like thick bush under the coconut trees. It turned out to be an avenue of red flamboyant trees dividing a ruined village of spectacularly derelict houses with rusted tin roofs and bulging walls. Some still had sagging verandas, and jalousies with mosquito wire, and improbable turrets and pinnacles. I went through a pair of fallen gateposts into what had once been a garden. The bougainvillea was tearing sheets from the roof, and there were huge hibiscus bushes with scarlet flowers and lemon and orange trees. I was so fascinated I nearly fell down an abandoned well, and for some reason that started me worrying about snakes so I went back to the main track. At the end, where mangrove began, was a stone cross reading Portugal 1140, 1640, 1940. The dates meant nothing to me, but there were the ruins of a little church with a bare cross that must have been English.

So this was the English colony. Beyond the mangrove was the sea but I couldn't find any track through and so turned left towards the harbour. There were little patches here of yams and sweet potato—incredible they could grow in mere sand dunes—and vines running everywhere with vivid purple flowers. Then the mangrove gave way, and I found myself starting at a beach washed by the waters of the Zambesi. It was littered with coconut husks and banana stems and strange twists of plant life, some with blue flowers still attached. There were hulks sunk in the sand, and one that seemed to serve as some sort of jetty. I stood there on a beach that seemed half sand, half rust, and watched a canoe pass upstream with six paddlers chanting in rhythm. As I followed its course, I turned to stare at the sunset, blazing a dozen versions of crimson and purple over the flat horizon with its lace-like coconut palms.

Just as, as the sun sank, the frogs started up, with an incredible battery of grunts and snuffles, far too varied to be just called croaking. I'd never heard them like this before and, of course, I started thinking of Mavuso.

I remembered my first reaction to Frog and Beauty, how they were bound together but moved independently. I still liked that, and of course I was wrong to see Beauty as an exploited woman, with no say in what was done to her. This wasn't social realism, it was a fable. Beauty was what's beautiful, created by Frog the poetical carver. The chief had power, with armies that could steal. But the birds and animals rose against him. And in the end, it was Frog the artist had the greater power. He could make and undo Beauty, restoring her to the original chunk of wood.

I had to go back. I had a degree to finish. But I'd added a link to my life. I was bound with people who'd never been mapmakers, missionaries, prospectors, big game hunters, stockbrokers, jobbers, commissioners, or dictators; people who cared not for nation or tribe but for the complex networks that are our common inheritance. Bound together, but moving separately. It's who I am.

Landeg White was born in South Wales. He taught at the University of the West Indies, Trinidad, where he was chief arranger for a steel band; in the University of Malawi, from where he was deported in 1972; in the University of Sierra Leone, where he wrote the detective novel *Inspector Tucker & the Leopard Men*, and in the University of Zambia, where he was teaching when his first book *V.S. Naipaul: a Critical Introduction*, appeared. He taught at the University of York where he joined the Centre for Southern African Studies, becoming Director in 1984. Here he wrote two Mozambican histories, the history of a village in Malawi, a study of southern Africa praise poetry, an anthology of African oral poetry (co-authored with Jack Mapanje) and three collections of his own poetry. Since 1994, he has lived in Portugal where he teaches at the *Universidade Aberta* (Open University). He has published a prize-winning translation of Camões' *The Lusiads,* and five further collections of poetry. *The Collected Lyrics of Luis de Camoes* was published by Princeton University Press in August (2008).